HERGÉ

THE ADVENTURES OF TINTIN

DESTINATION MOON

LITTLE, BROWN AND COMPANY

BOSTON/NEW YORK/TORONTO/LONDON

Translated by Leslie Lonsdale-Cooper
and Michael Turner

The TINTIN books are published in the following languages :

Afrikaans :		HUMAN & ROUSSEAU, Cape Town.
Arabic :		DAR AL-MAAREF, Cairo.
Basque :		MENSAJERO, Bilbao.
Brazilian :		DISTRIBUIDORA RECORD, Rio de Janeiro.
Breton :		CASTERMAN, Paris.
Catalan :		JUVENTUD, Barcelona.
Chinese :		EPOCH, Taipei.
Danish :		CARLSEN IF, Copenhagen.
Dutch :		CASTERMAN, Dronten.
English :	U.K. :	METHUEN CHILDREN'S BOOKS, London.
	Australia :	REED PUBLISHING AUSTRALIA, Melbourne.
	Canada :	REED PUBLISHING CANADA, Toronto.
	New Zealand :	REED PUBLISHING NEW ZEALAND, Auckland.
	Republic of South Africa :	STRUIK BOOK DISTRIBUTORS, Johannesburg.
	Singapore :	REED PUBLISHING ASIA, Singapore.
	Spain :	EDICIONES DEL PRADO, Madrid.
	Portugal :	EDICIONES DEL PRADO, Madrid.
	U.S.A.	LITTLE BROWN, Boston.
Esperanto :		CASTERMAN, Paris.
Finnish :		OTAVA, Helsinki.
French :		CASTERMAN, Paris-Tournai.
	Spain :	EDICIONES DEL PRADO, Madrid.
	Portugal :	EDICIONES DEL PRADO, Madrid.
Galician :		JUVENTUD, Barcelona.
German :		CARLSEN, Reinbek-Hamburg.
Greek :		ANGLO-HELLENIC, Athens.
Icelandic :		FJÖLVI, Reykjavik.
Indonesian :		INDIRA, Jakarta.
Iranian :		MODERN PRINTING HOUSE, Teheran.
Italian :		GANDUS, Genoa.
Japanese :		FUKUINKAN SHOTEN, Tokyo.
Korean :		UNIVERSAL PUBLICATIONS, Seoul.
Malay :		SHARIKAT UNITED, Pulau Pinang.
Norwegian :		SEMIC, Oslo.
Picard :		CASTERMAN, Paris.
Portuguese :		CENTRO DO LIVRO BRASILEIRO, Lisboa.
Provençal :		CASTERMAN, Paris.
Spanish :		JUVENTUD, Barcelona.
	Argentina :	JUVENTUD ARGENTINA, Buenos Aires.
	Mexico :	MARIN, Mexico.
	Peru :	DISTR. DE LIBROS DEL PACIFICO, Lima.
Serbo-Croatian :		DECJE NOVINE, Gornji Milanovac.
Swedish :		CARLSEN IF, Stockholm.
Welsh :		GWASG Y DREF WEN, Cardiff.

Library of Congress Catalogue Card Number Afo 12985

Library of Congress Catalogue Card Number R 104022

Library of Congress catalog card no. 76-13279
20 19 18 17

Published pursuant to agreement with Casterman, Paris
Not for sale in the British Commonwealth
Printed in Spain

DESTINATION MOON

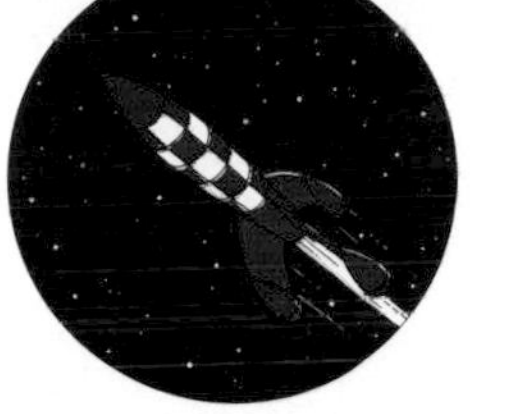

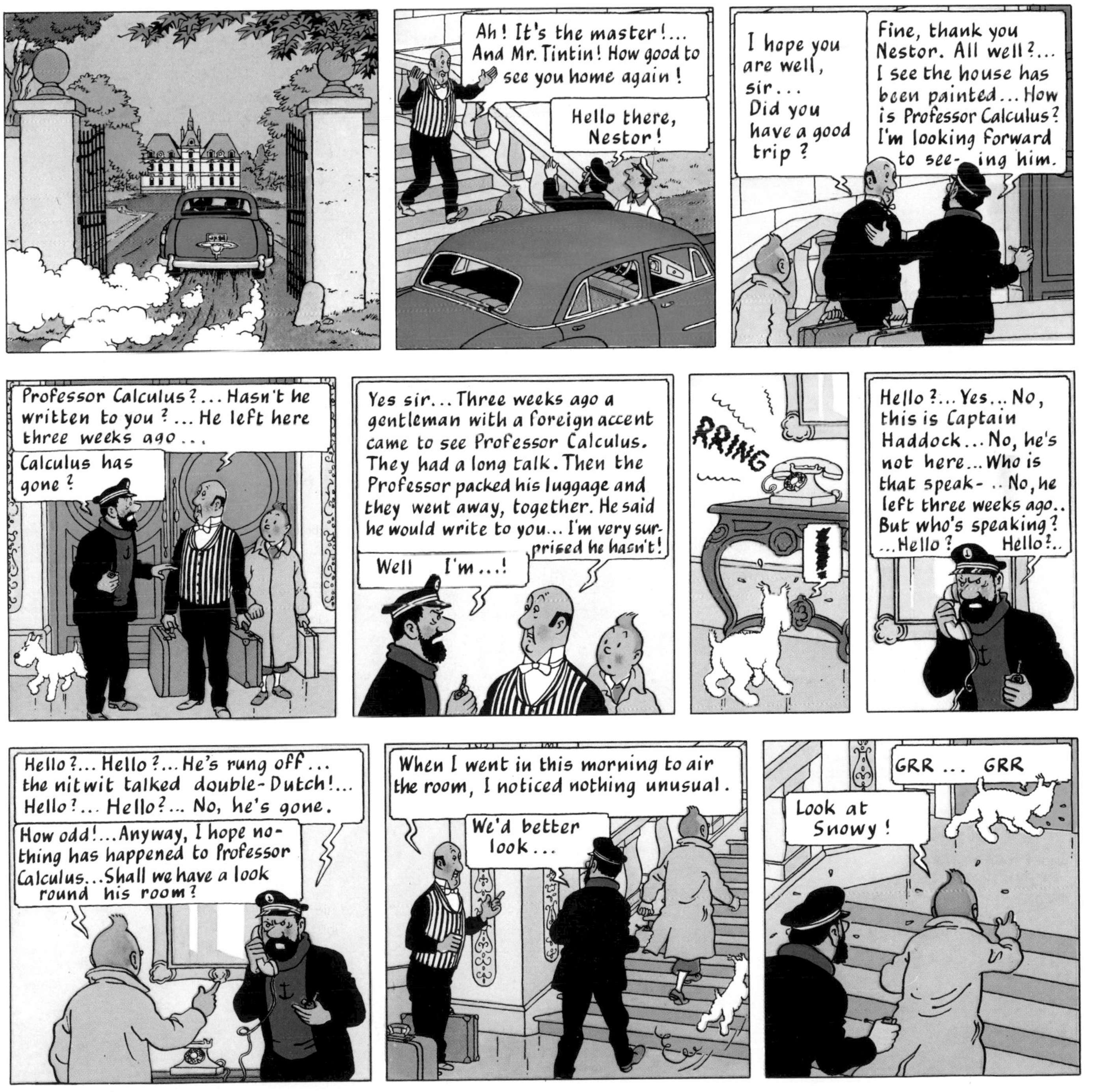

Ah! It's the master!... And Mr. Tintin! How good to see you home again!
Hello there, Nestor!
I hope you are well, sir... Did you have a good trip?
Fine, thank you Nestor. All well?... I see the house has been painted... How is Professor Calculus? I'm looking forward to see- ing him.
Professor Calculus?... Hasn't he written to you?... He left here three weeks ago...
Calculus has gone?
Yes sir... Three weeks ago a gentleman with a foreign accent came to see Professor Calculus. They had a long talk. Then the Professor packed his luggage and they went away, together. He said he would write to you... I'm very sur- prised he hasn't!
Well I'm...!
RRING
Hello?... Yes... No, this is Captain Haddock... No, he's not here... Who is that speak- .. No, he left three weeks ago.. But who's speaking? ...Hello? Hello?..
Hello?... Hello?... He's rung off... the nitwit talked double-Dutch!... Hello?... Hello?... No, he's gone.
How odd!... Anyway, I hope nothing has happened to Professor Calculus... Shall we have a look round his room?
When I went in this morning to air the room, I noticed nothing unusual.
We'd better look...
GRR ... GRR
Look at Snowy!

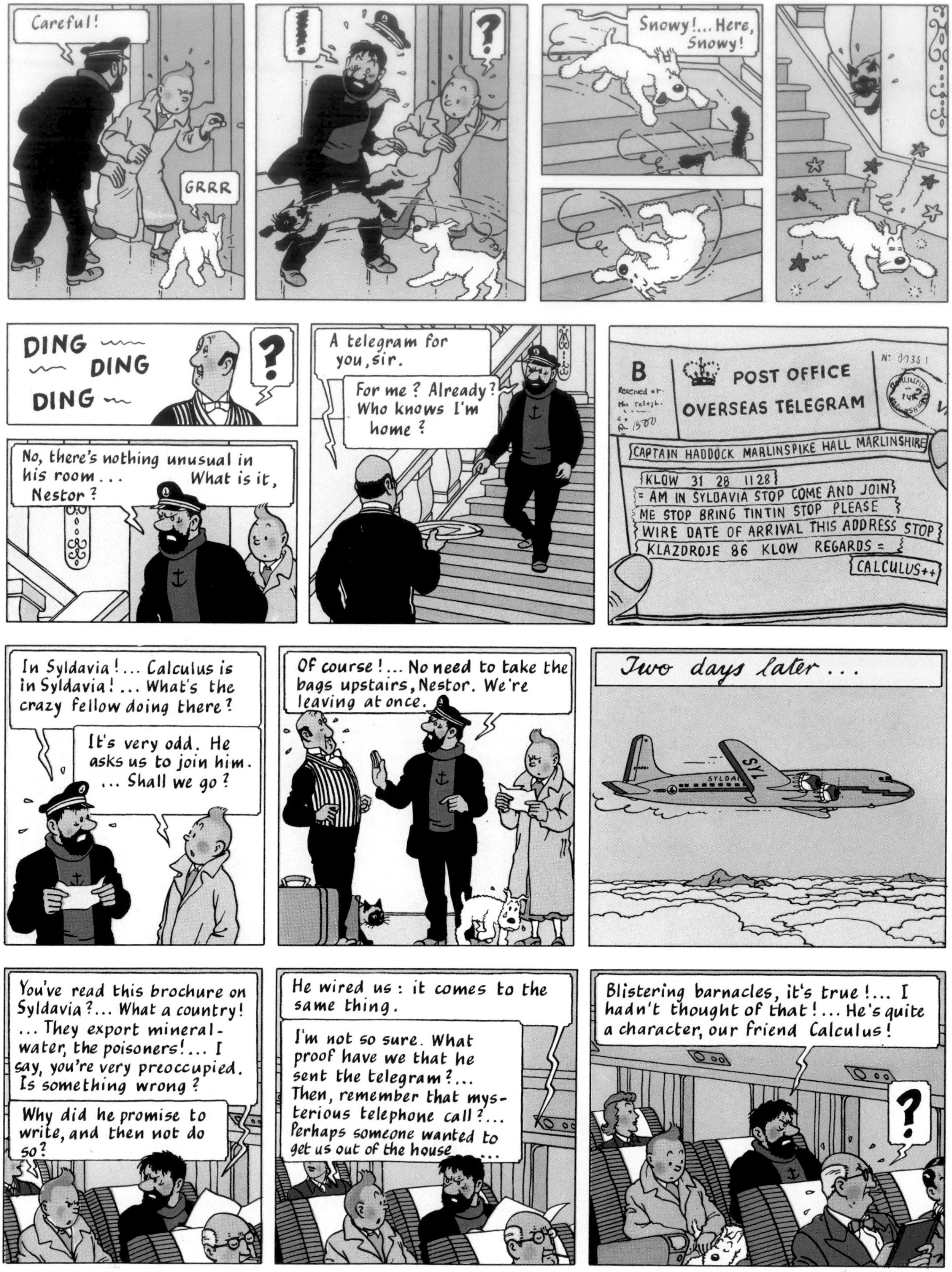

Careful!
GRRR
!
?
Snowy!... Here, Snowy!
DING DING DING
?
No, there's nothing unusual in his room... What is it, Nestor?
A telegram for you, sir.
For me? Already? Who knows I'm home?
B
POST OFFICE
OVERSEAS TELEGRAM
CAPTAIN HADDOCK MARLINSPIKE HALL MARLINSHIRE
KLOW 31 28 1128
= AM IN SYLDAVIA STOP COME AND JOIN
ME STOP BRING TINTIN STOP PLEASE
WIRE DATE OF ARRIVAL THIS ADDRESS STOP
KLAZDROJE 86 KLOW REGARDS =
CALCULUS++
In Syldavia!... Calculus is in Syldavia!... What's the crazy fellow doing there?
It's very odd. He asks us to join him. ... Shall we go?
Of course!... No need to take the bags upstairs, Nestor. We're leaving at once.
Two days later...
SYL
You've read this brochure on Syldavia?... What a country! ... They export mineral-water, the poisoners!... I say, you're very preoccupied. Is something wrong?
Why did he promise to write, and then not do so?
He wired us: it comes to the same thing.
I'm not so sure. What proof have we that he sent the telegram?... Then, remember that mysterious telephone call?... Perhaps someone wanted to get us out of the house...
Blistering barnacles, it's true!... I hadn't thought of that!... He's quite a character, our friend Calculus!
?

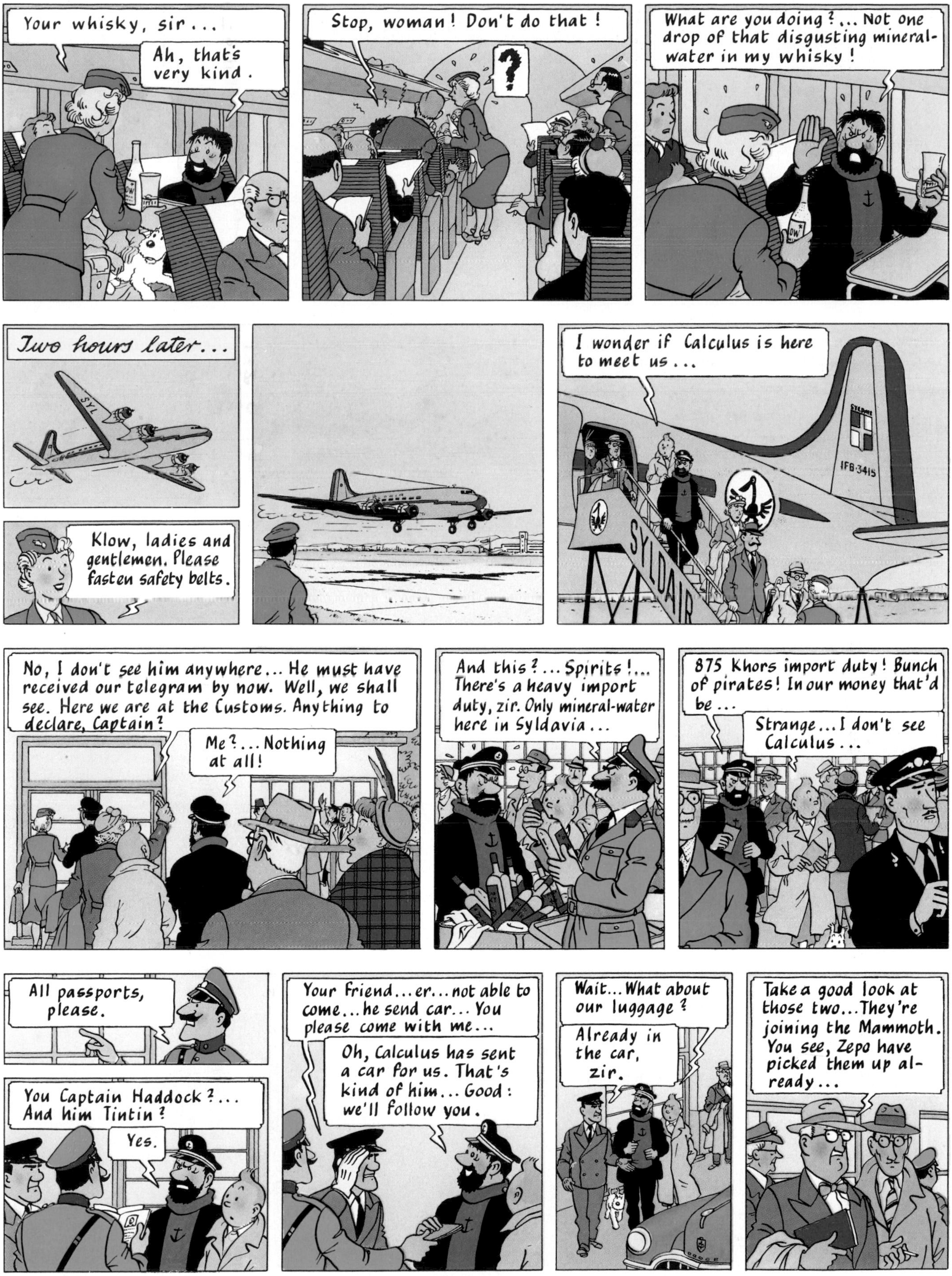
Your whisky, sir...
Ah, that's very kind.
Stop, woman! Don't do that!
?
What are you doing?... Not one drop of that disgusting mineral-water in my whisky!
Two hours later...
SYL
Klow, ladies and gentlemen. Please fasten safety belts.
I wonder if Calculus is here to meet us...
1FB-3415
SYLDAIR
No, I don't see him anywhere... He must have received our telegram by now. Well, we shall see. Here we are at the Customs. Anything to declare, Captain?
Me?... Nothing at all!
And this?... Spirits!... There's a heavy import duty, zir. Only mineral-water here in Syldavia...
875 Khors import duty! Bunch of pirates! In our money that'd be...
Strange... I don't see Calculus...
All passports, please.
You Captain Haddock?... And him Tintin?
Yes.
Your friend... er... not able to come... he send car... You please come with me...
Oh, Calculus has sent a car for us. That's kind of him... Good: we'll follow you.
Wait... What about our luggage?
Already in the car, zir.
Take a good look at those two... They're joining the Mammoth. You see, Zepo have picked them up already...

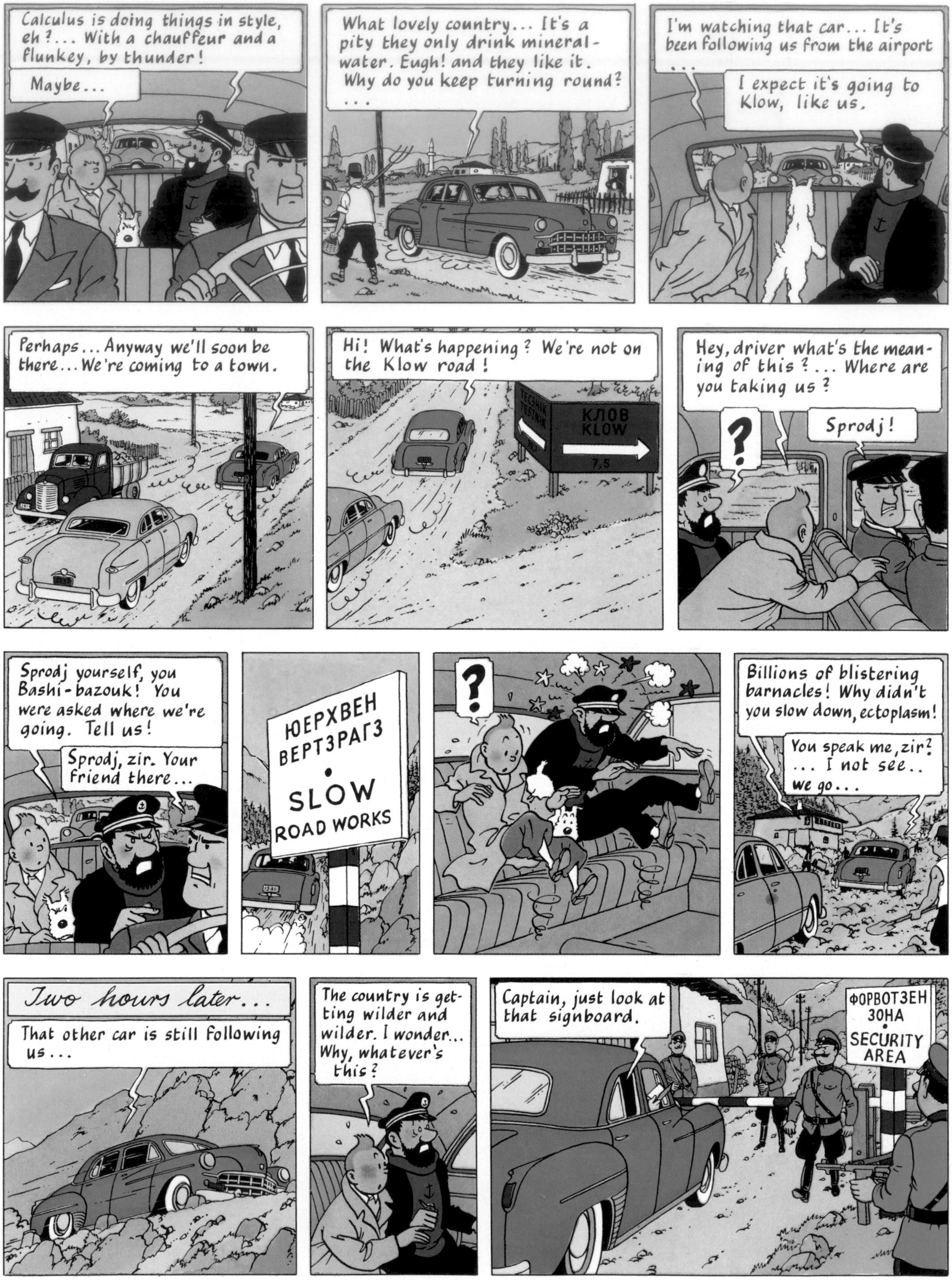

Calculus is doing things in style, eh?... With a chauffeur and a flunkey, by thunder!
Maybe...
What lovely country... It's a pity they only drink mineral-water. Eugh! and they like it. Why do you keep turning round?...
I'm watching that car... It's been following us from the airport...
I expect it's going to Klow, like us.
Perhaps... Anyway we'll soon be there... We're coming to a town.
Hi! What's happening? We're not on the Klow road!
КЛОВ
KLOW
7,5
Hey, driver what's the meaning of this?... Where are you taking us?
?
Sprodj!
Sprodj yourself, you Bashi-bazouk! You were asked where we're going. Tell us!
Sprodj, zir. Your friend there...
ЮЕРХВЕН
ВЕРТЗРАГЗ
SLOW
ROAD WORKS
?
Billions of blistering barnacles! Why didn't you slow down, ectoplasm!
You speak me, zir? ... I not see.. we go...
Two hours later...
That other car is still following us...
The country is getting wilder and wilder. I wonder... Why, whatever's this?
Captain, just look at that signboard.
ФОРВОТЗЕН
ЗОНА
SECURITY
AREA

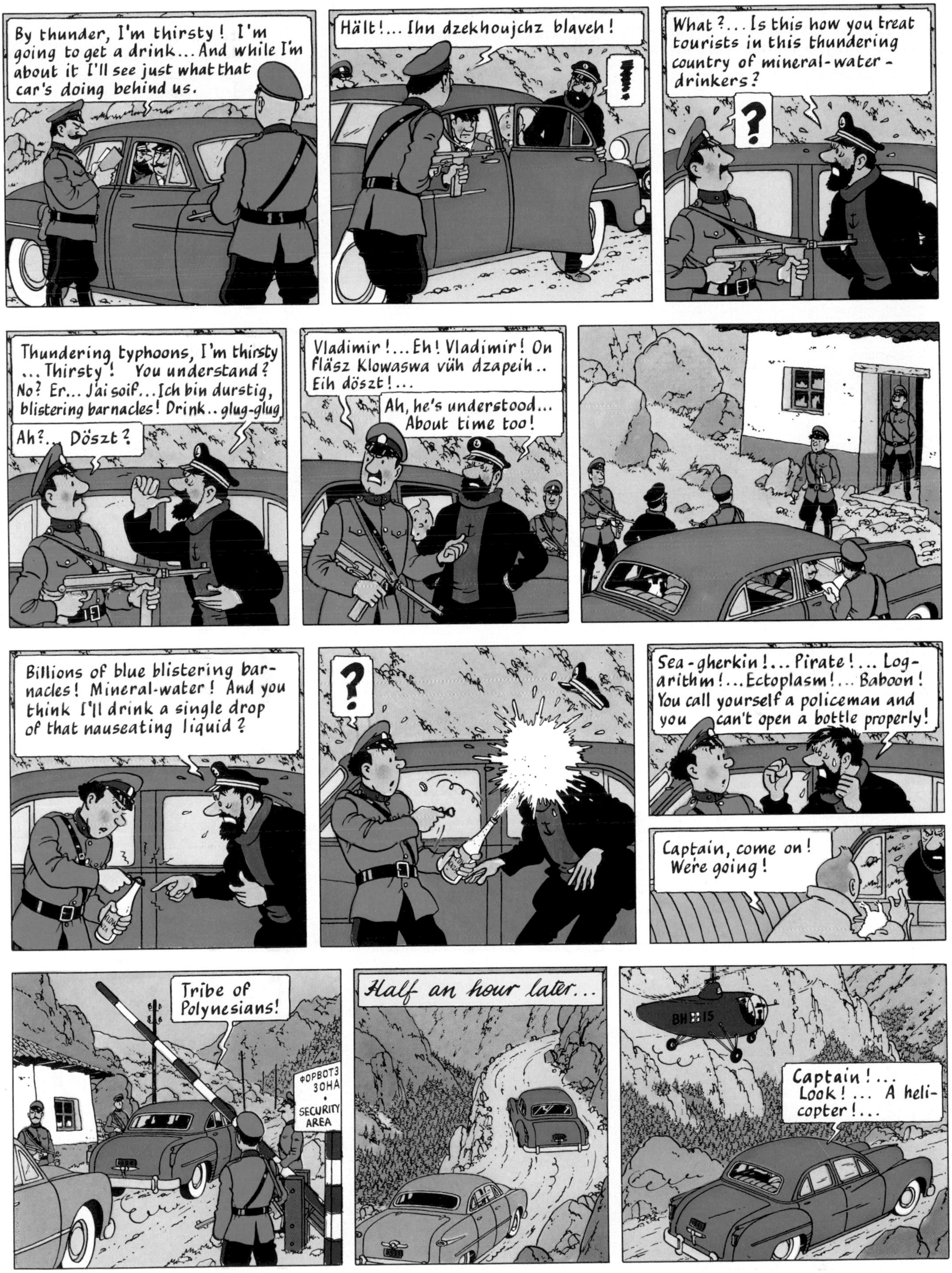

By thunder, I'm thirsty! I'm going to get a drink... And while I'm about it I'll see just what that car's doing behind us.
Hält!... Ihn dzekhoujchz blaveh!
What?... Is this how you treat tourists in this thundering country of mineral-water-drinkers?
?
Thundering typhoons, I'm thirsty ... Thirsty! You understand? No? Er... J'ai soif... Ich bin durstig, blistering barnacles! Drink.. glug-glug
Ah?... Döszt?
Vladimir!... Eh! Vladimir! On fläsz Klowaswa vüh dzapeih.. Eih döszt!...
Ah, he's understood... About time too!
Billions of blue blistering barnacles! Mineral-water! And you think I'll drink a single drop of that nauseating liquid?
?
Sea-gherkin!... Pirate!... Logarithm!... Ectoplasm!... Baboon! You call yourself a policeman and you can't open a bottle properly!
Captain, come on! We're going!
Tribe of Polynesians!
ФОРВОТЗ ЗОНА
SECURITY AREA
Half an hour later...
BH 15
Captain!... Look!... A helicopter!...

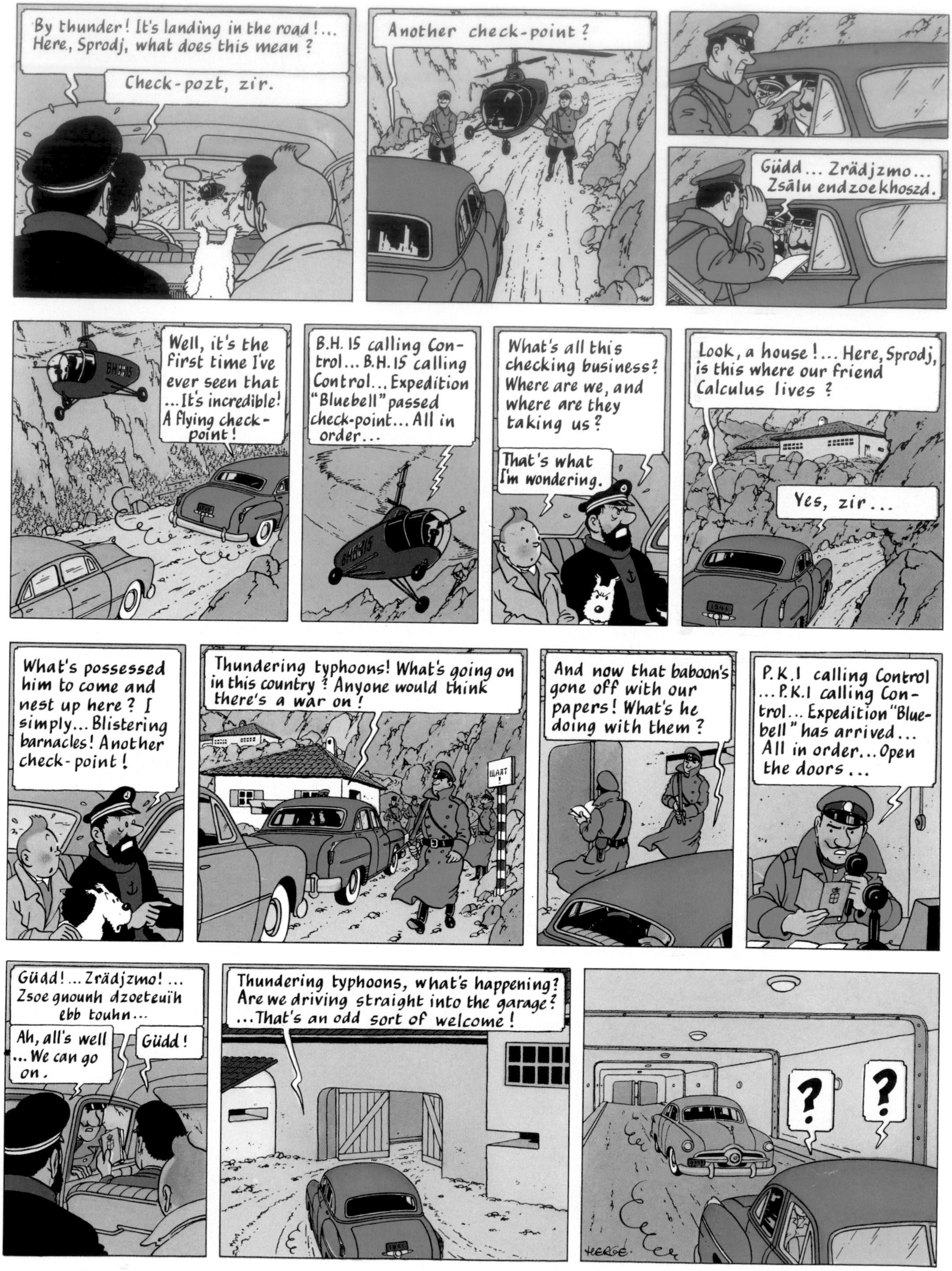

By thunder! It's landing in the road!... Here, Sprodj, what does this mean?
Check-pozt, zir.
Another check-point?
Güdd... Zrädjzmo... Zsālu endzoekhoszd.
Well, it's the first time I've ever seen that ...It's incredible! A flying check-point!
B.H.15 calling Control... B.H.15 calling Control... Expedition "Bluebell" passed check-point... All in order...
What's all this checking business? Where are we, and where are they taking us?
That's what I'm wondering.
Look, a house!... Here, Sprodj, is this where our friend Calculus lives?
Yes, zir...
What's possessed him to come and nest up here? I simply... Blistering barnacles! Another check-point!
Thundering typhoons! What's going on in this country? Anyone would think there's a war on!
And now that baboon's gone off with our papers! What's he doing with them?
P.K.1 calling Control ...P.K.1 calling Control... Expedition "Bluebell" has arrived... All in order... Open the doors...
Güdd!... Zrädjzmo!... Zsoe gnounh dzoeteuïh ebb touhn...
Ah, all's well ...We can go on.
Güdd!
Thundering typhoons, what's happening? Are we driving straight into the garage? ...That's an odd sort of welcome!
?
?

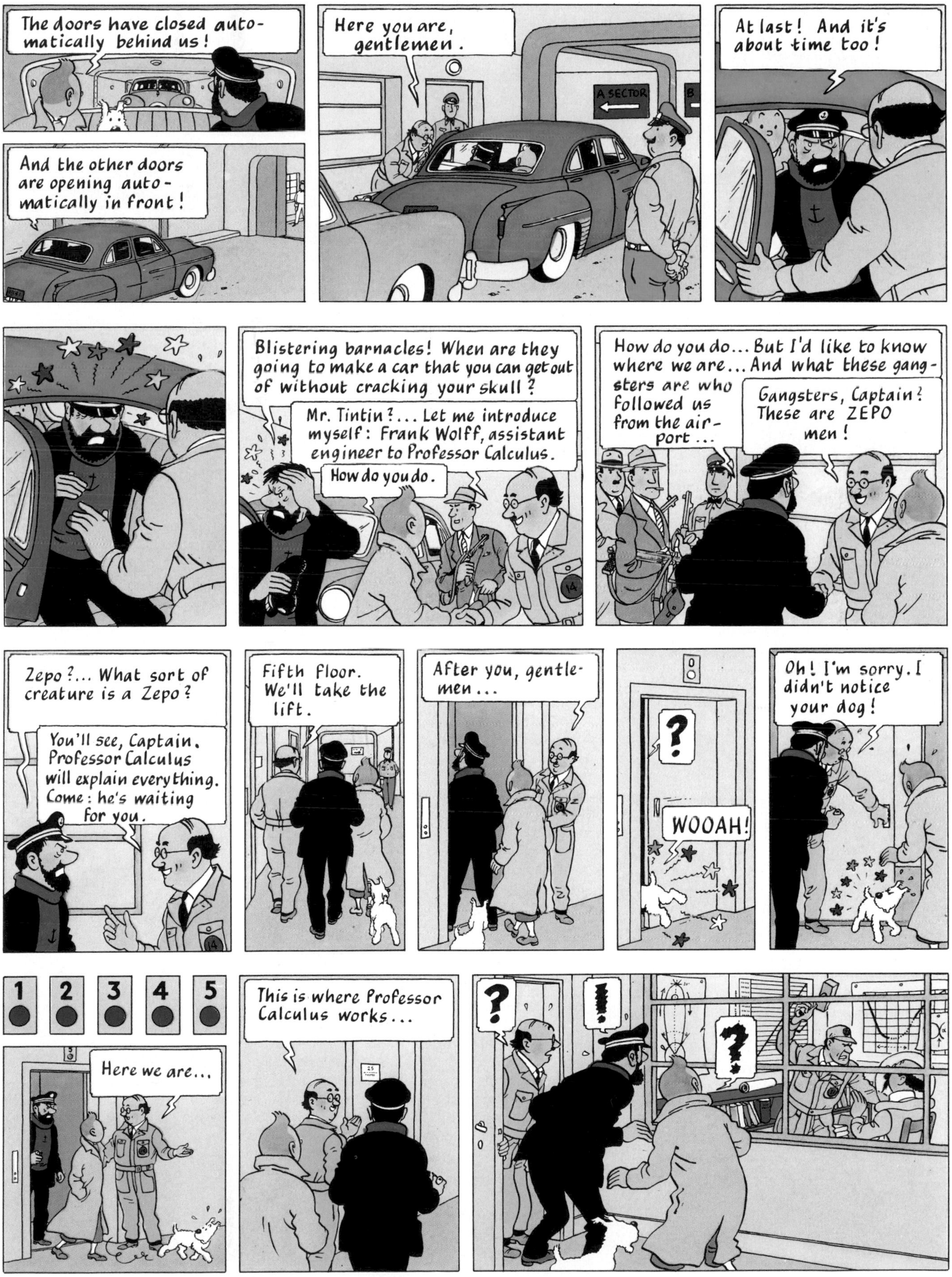
The doors have closed automatically behind us!
And the other doors are opening automatically in front!
Here you are, gentlemen.
A SECTOR
B
At last! And it's about time too!
Blistering barnacles! When are they going to make a car that you can get out of without cracking your skull?
Mr. Tintin?... Let me introduce myself: Frank Wolff, assistant engineer to Professor Calculus.
How do you do.
How do you do... But I'd like to know where we are... And what these gangsters are who followed us from the airport...
Gangsters, Captain? These are ZEPO men!
Zepo?... What sort of creature is a Zepo?
You'll see, Captain. Professor Calculus will explain everything. Come: he's waiting for you.
Fifth floor. We'll take the lift.
After you, gentlemen...
?
WOOAH!
Oh! I'm sorry. I didn't notice your dog!
1 2 3 4 5
Here we are...
This is where Professor Calculus works...
?
!
?

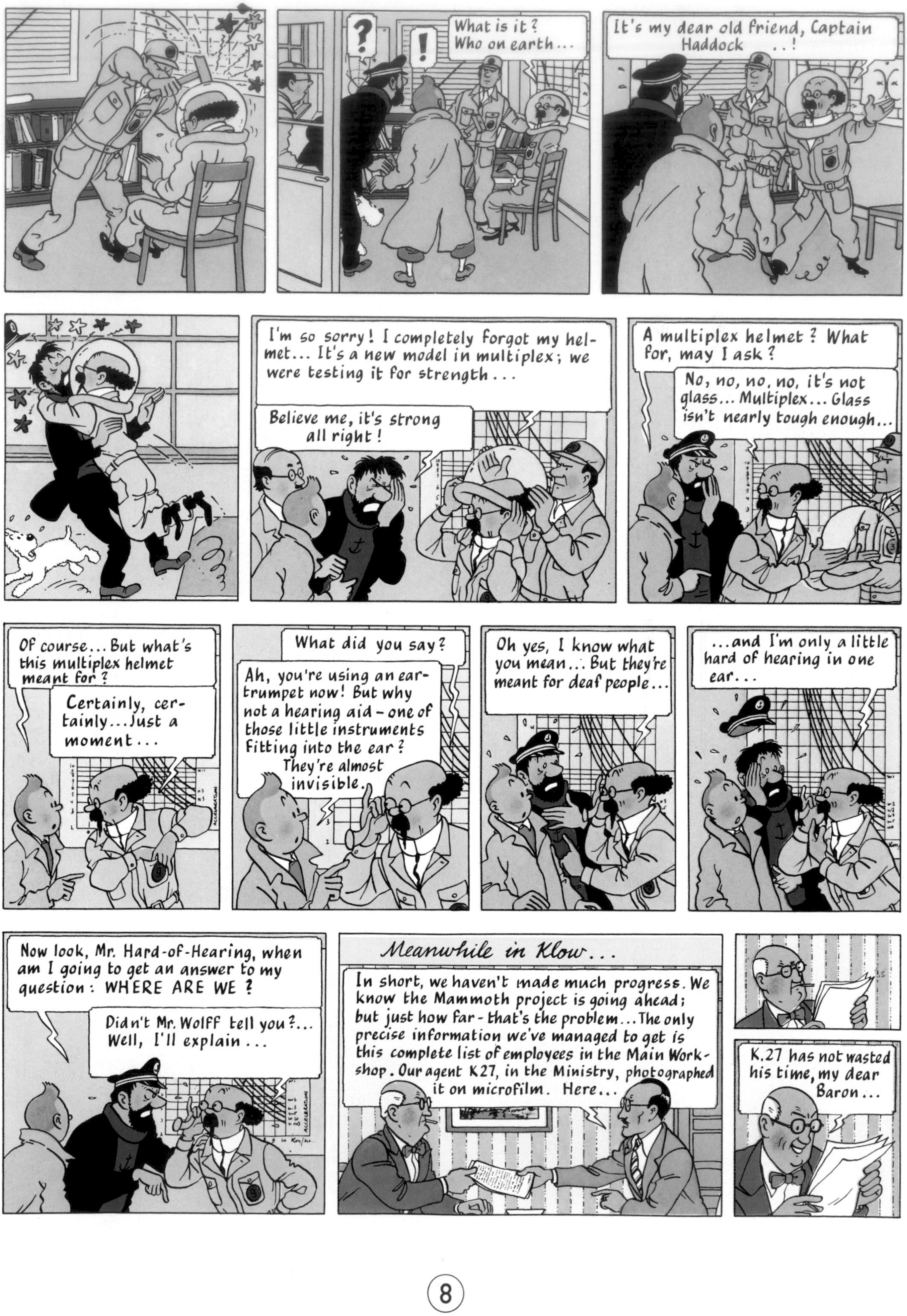
What is it? Who on earth...
It's my dear old friend, Captain Haddock ..!
I'm so sorry! I completely forgot my helmet... It's a new model in multiplex; we were testing it for strength...
Believe me, it's strong all right!
A multiplex helmet? What for, may I ask?
No, no, no, no, it's not glass... Multiplex... Glass isn't nearly tough enough...
Of course... But what's this multiplex helmet meant for?
Certainly, certainly... Just a moment...
What did you say?
Ah, you're using an ear-trumpet now! But why not a hearing aid - one of those little instruments fitting into the ear? They're almost invisible.
Oh yes, I know what you mean... But they're meant for deaf people...
...and I'm only a little hard of hearing in one ear...
Now look, Mr. Hard-of-Hearing, when am I going to get an answer to my question: WHERE ARE WE?
Didn't Mr. Wolff tell you?... Well, I'll explain...
Meanwhile in Klow...
In short, we haven't made much progress. We know the Mammoth project is going ahead; but just how far - that's the problem... The only precise information we've managed to get is this complete list of employees in the Main Workshop. Our agent K27, in the Ministry, photographed it on microfilm. Here...
K.27 has not wasted his time, my dear Baron...

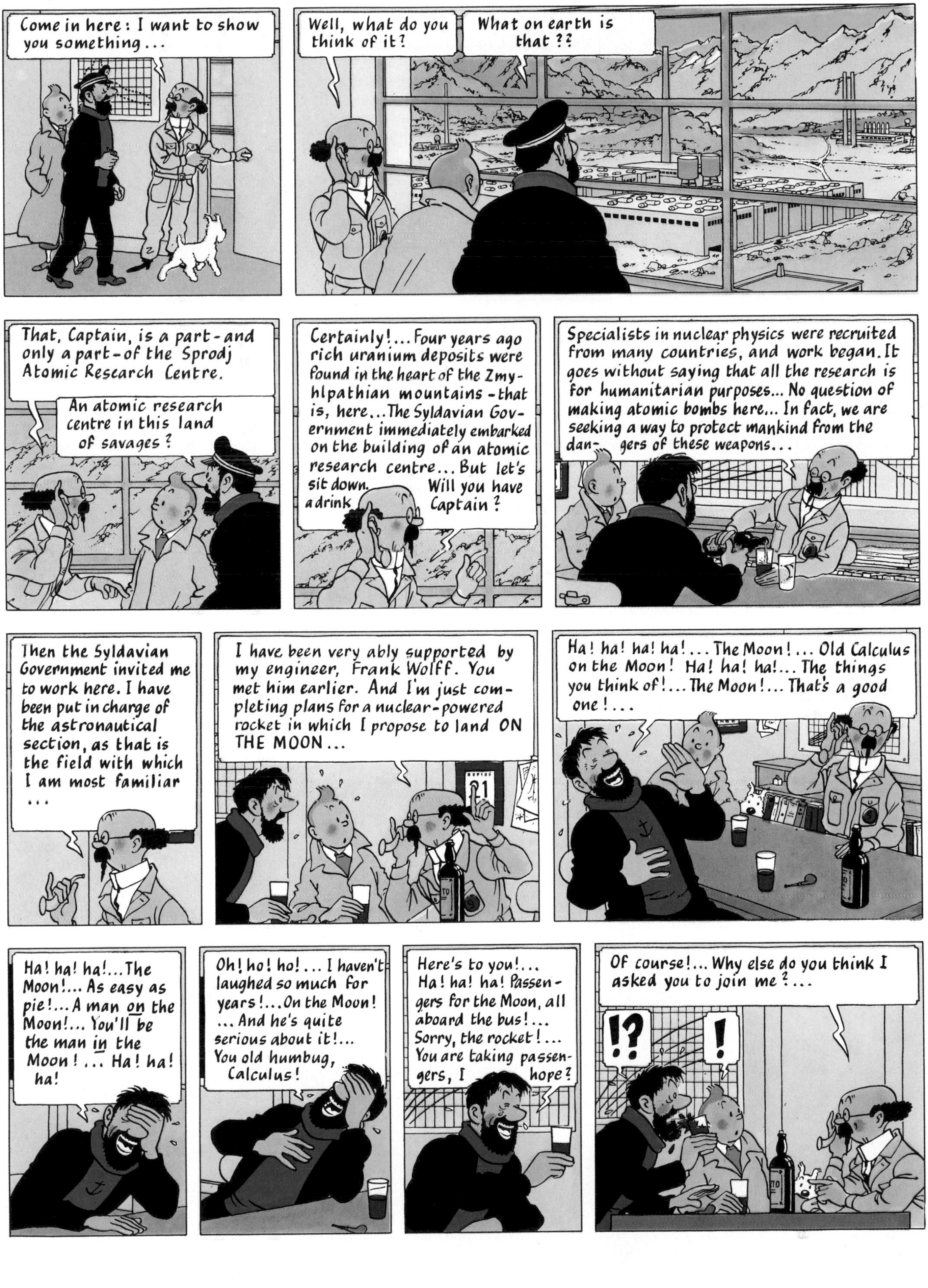
Come in here: I want to show you something...
Well, what do you think of it?
What on earth is that ??
That, Captain, is a part - and only a part - of the Sprodj Atomic Research Centre.
An atomic research centre in this land of savages ?
Certainly!... Four years ago rich uranium deposits were found in the heart of the Zmyhlpathian mountains - that is, here... The Syldavian Government immediately embarked on the building of an atomic research centre... But let's sit down. Will you have a drink Captain ?
Specialists in nuclear physics were recruited from many countries, and work began. It goes without saying that all the research is for humanitarian purposes... No question of making atomic bombs here... In fact, we are seeking a way to protect mankind from the dangers of these weapons...
Then the Syldavian Government invited me to work here. I have been put in charge of the astronautical section, as that is the field with which I am most familiar ...
I have been very ably supported by my engineer, Frank Wolff. You met him earlier. And I'm just completing plans for a nuclear-powered rocket in which I propose to land ON THE MOON...
Ha! ha! ha! ha!... The Moon!... Old Calculus on the Moon! Ha! ha! ha!... The things you think of!... The Moon!... That's a good one!...
Ha! ha! ha!... The Moon!... As easy as pie!... A man on the Moon!... You'll be the man in the Moon!... Ha! ha! ha!
Oh! ho! ho!... I haven't laughed so much for years!... On the Moon! ... And he's quite serious about it!... You old humbug, Calculus!
Here's to you!... Ha! ha! ha! Passengers for the Moon, all aboard the bus!... Sorry, the rocket!... You are taking passengers, I hope?
Of course!... Why else do you think I asked you to join me?...
!?
!

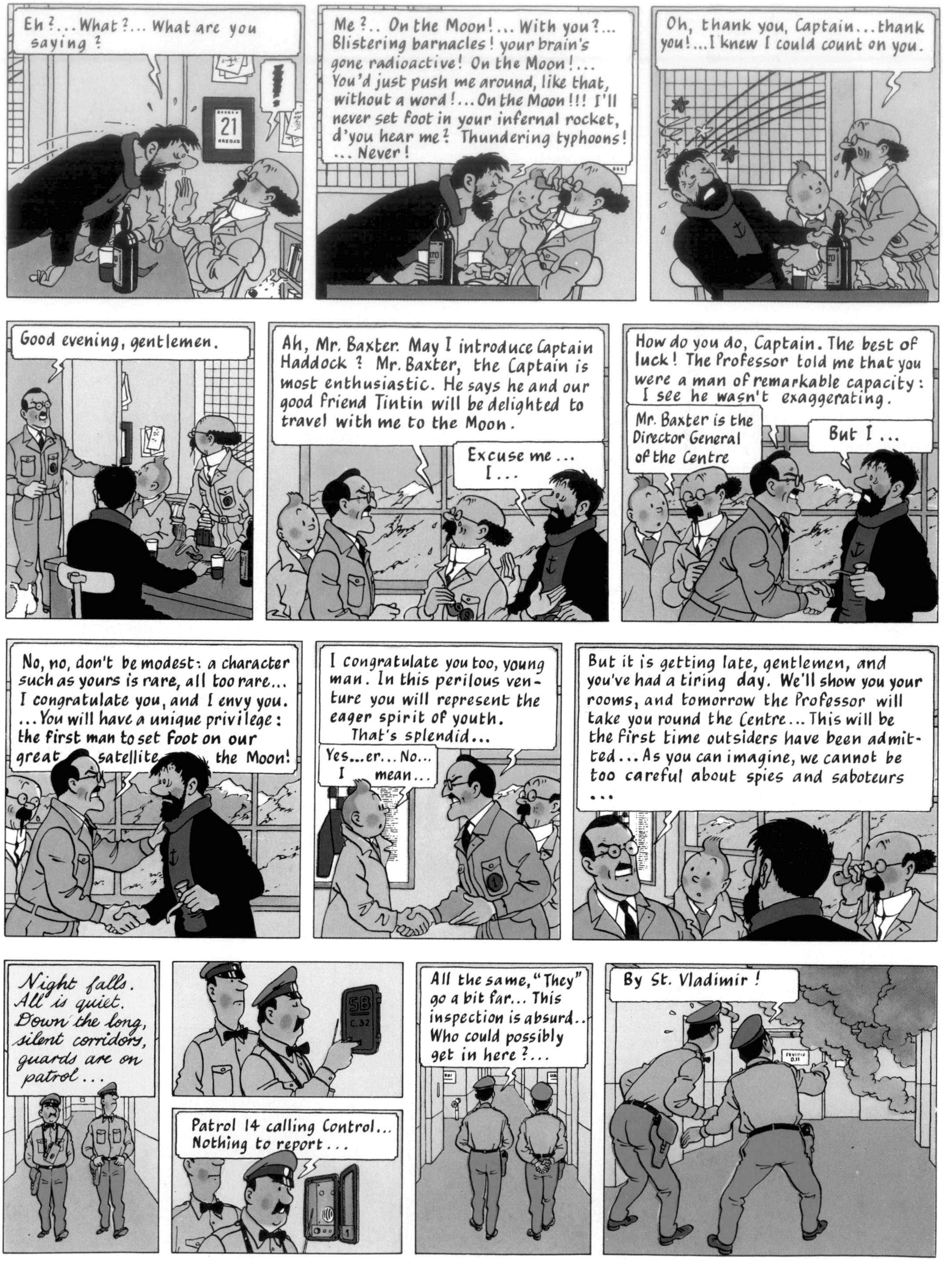

Eh?... What?... What are you saying?
Me?.. On the Moon!... With you?... Blistering barnacles! your brain's gone radioactive! On the Moon!... You'd just push me around, like that, without a word!... On the Moon!!! I'll never set foot in your infernal rocket, d'you hear me? Thundering typhoons! ... Never!
Oh, thank you, Captain... thank you!... I knew I could count on you.
Good evening, gentlemen.
Ah, Mr. Baxter. May I introduce Captain Haddock? Mr. Baxter, the Captain is most enthusiastic. He says he and our good friend Tintin will be delighted to travel with me to the Moon.
Excuse me... I...
How do you do, Captain. The best of luck! The Professor told me that you were a man of remarkable capacity: I see he wasn't exaggerating.
Mr. Baxter is the Director General of the Centre
But I...
No, no, don't be modest: a character such as yours is rare, all too rare... I congratulate you, and I envy you. ... You will have a unique privilege: the first man to set foot on our great satellite the Moon!
I congratulate you too, young man. In this perilous venture you will represent the eager spirit of youth. That's splendid...
Yes...er... No... I mean...
But it is getting late, gentlemen, and you've had a tiring day. We'll show you your rooms, and tomorrow the Professor will take you round the Centre... This will be the first time outsiders have been admitted... As you can imagine, we cannot be too careful about spies and saboteurs ...
Night falls. All is quiet. Down the long, silent corridors, guards are on patrol...
SB C.32
Patrol 14 calling Control... Nothing to report...
All the same, "They" go a bit far... This inspection is absurd.. Who could possibly get in here?...
By St. Vladimir!

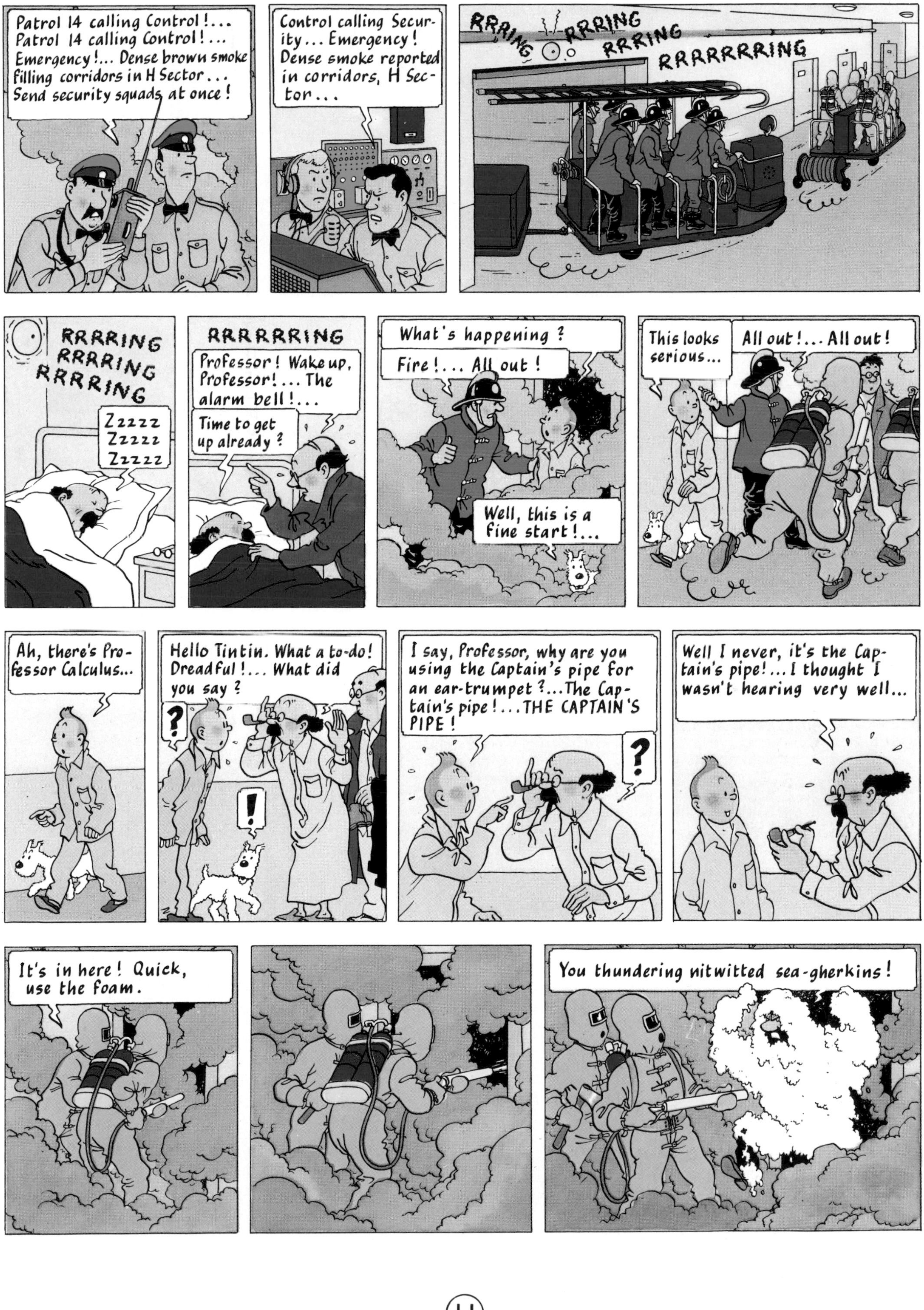
Patrol 14 calling Control!... Patrol 14 calling Control!... Emergency!... Dense brown smoke filling corridors in H Sector... Send security squads at once!
Control calling Security... Emergency! Dense smoke reported in corridors, H Sector...
RRRING RRRING RRRING RRRRRRRING
RRRRING RRRRING RRRRING
Zzzzz Zzzzz Zzzzz
RRRRRRRING
Professor! Wake up, Professor!... The alarm bell!...
Time to get up already?
What's happening?
Fire!... All out!
Well, this is a fine start!...
This looks serious...
All out!... All out!
Ah, there's Professor Calculus...
Hello Tintin. What a to-do! Dreadful!... What did you say?
?
!
I say, Professor, why are you using the Captain's pipe for an ear-trumpet?...The Captain's pipe!... THE CAPTAIN'S PIPE!
?
Well I never, it's the Captain's pipe!... I thought I wasn't hearing very well...
It's in here! Quick, use the foam.
You thundering nitwitted sea-gherkins!

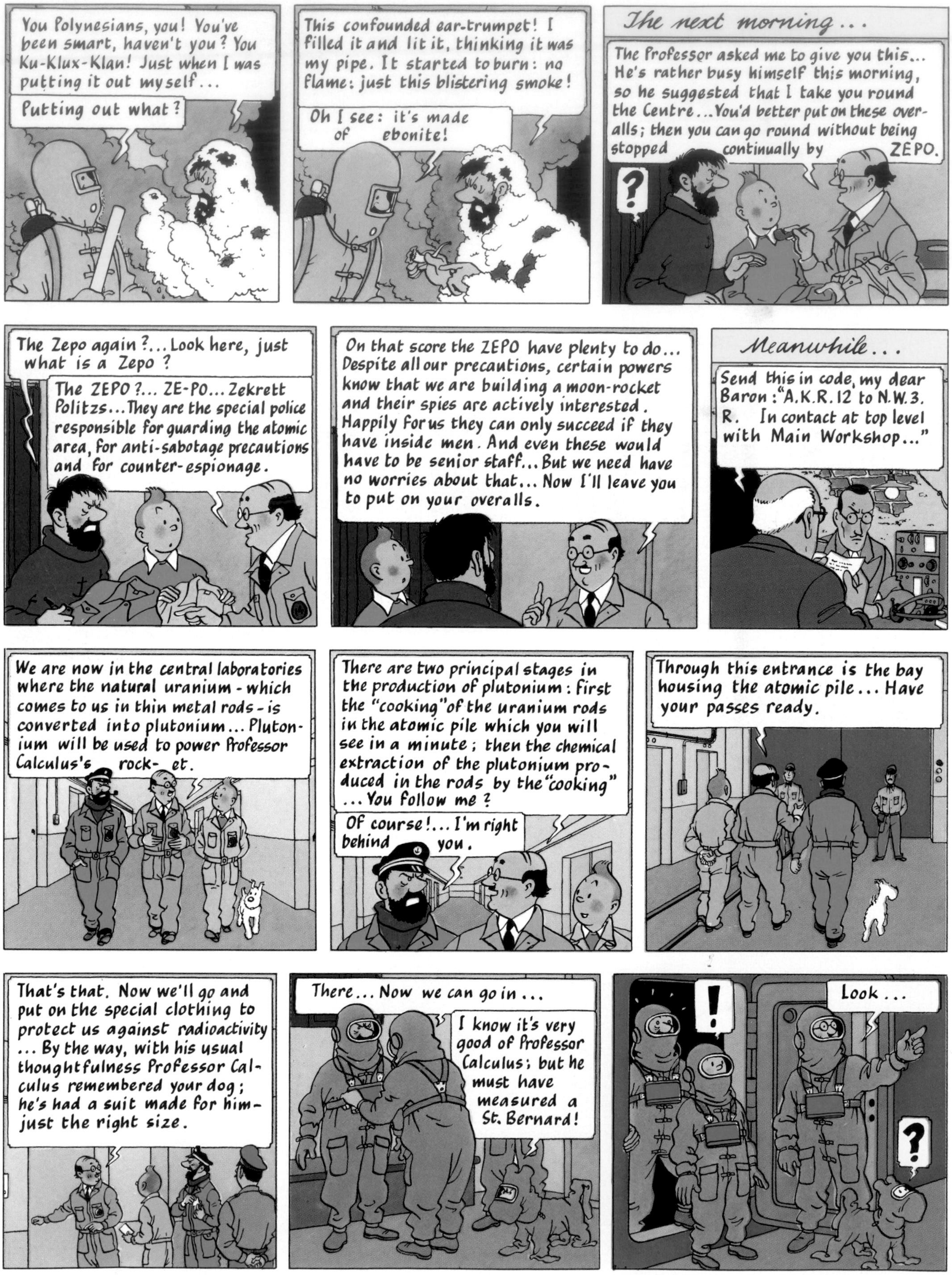
You Polynesians, you! You've been smart, haven't you? You Ku-Klux-Klan! Just when I was putting it out myself...
Putting out what?
This confounded ear-trumpet! I filled it and lit it, thinking it was my pipe. It started to burn: no flame: just this blistering smoke!
Oh I see: it's made of ebonite!
The next morning...
The Professor asked me to give you this... He's rather busy himself this morning, so he suggested that I take you round the Centre... You'd better put on these overalls; then you can go round without being stopped continually by ZEPO.
?
The Zepo again?... Look here, just what is a Zepo?
The ZEPO?... ZE-PO... Zekrett Politzs... They are the special police responsible for guarding the atomic area, for anti-sabotage precautions and for counter-espionage.
On that score the ZEPO have plenty to do... Despite all our precautions, certain powers know that we are building a moon-rocket and their spies are actively interested. Happily for us they can only succeed if they have inside men. And even these would have to be senior staff... But we need have no worries about that... Now I'll leave you to put on your overalls.
Meanwhile...
Send this in code, my dear Baron: "A.K.R. 12 to N.W.3. R. In contact at top level with Main Workshop..."
We are now in the central laboratories where the natural uranium - which comes to us in thin metal rods - is converted into plutonium... Plutonium will be used to power Professor Calculus's rock-et.
There are two principal stages in the production of plutonium: first the "cooking" of the uranium rods in the atomic pile which you will see in a minute; then the chemical extraction of the plutonium produced in the rods by the "cooking"... You follow me?
Of course!... I'm right behind you.
Through this entrance is the bay housing the atomic pile... Have your passes ready.
That's that. Now we'll go and put on the special clothing to protect us against radioactivity... By the way, with his usual thoughtfulness Professor Calculus remembered your dog; he's had a suit made for him - just the right size.
There... Now we can go in...
I know it's very good of Professor Calculus; but he must have measured a St. Bernard!
!
Look...
?

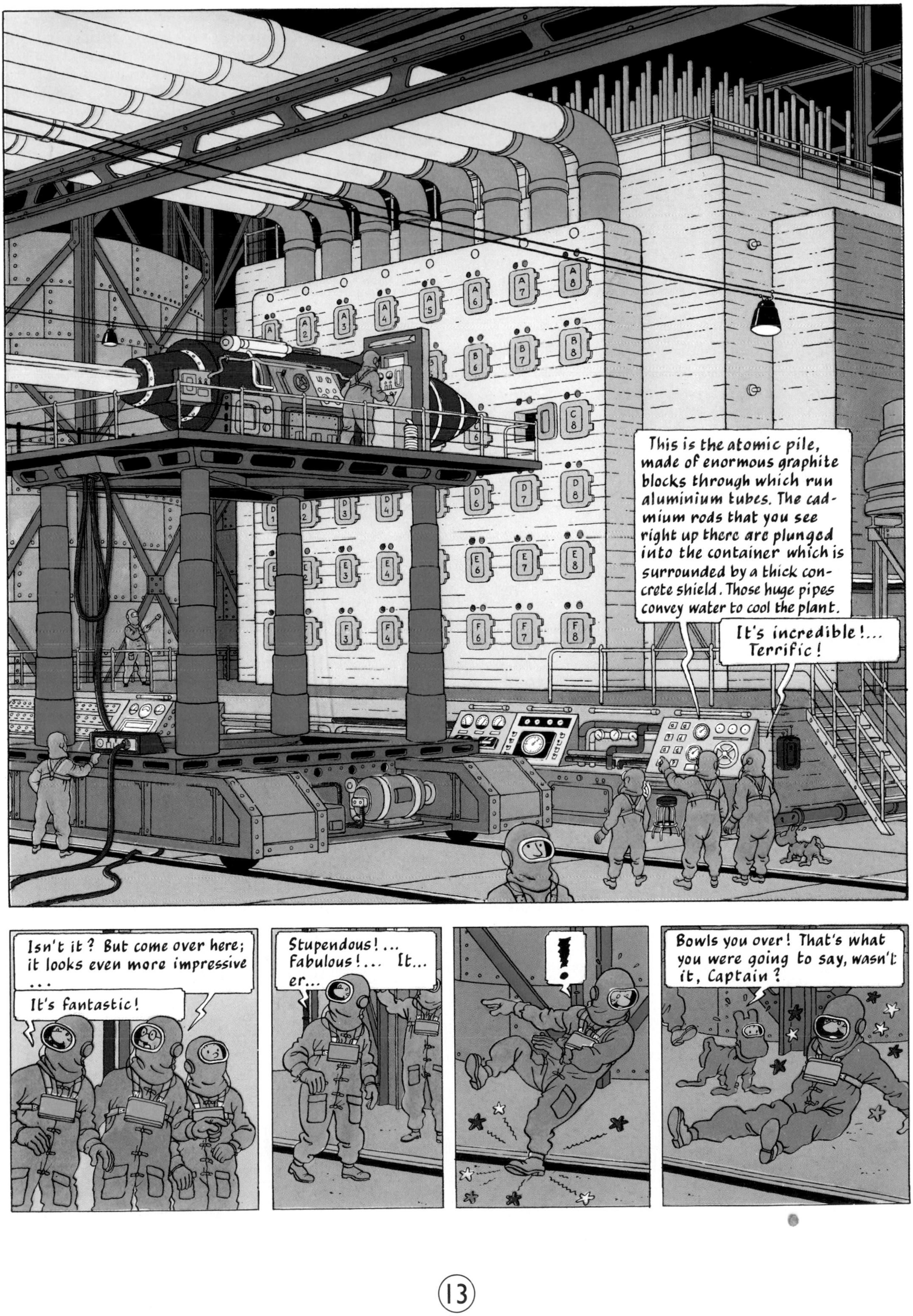
This is the atomic pile, made of enormous graphite blocks through which run aluminium tubes. The cadmium rods that you see right up there are plunged into the container which is surrounded by a thick concrete shield. Those huge pipes convey water to cool the plant.
It's incredible!... Terrific!
Isn't it? But come over here; it looks even more impressive ...
It's fantastic!
Stupendous!... Fabulous!... It... er...
!
Bowls you over! That's what you were going to say, wasn't it, Captain?

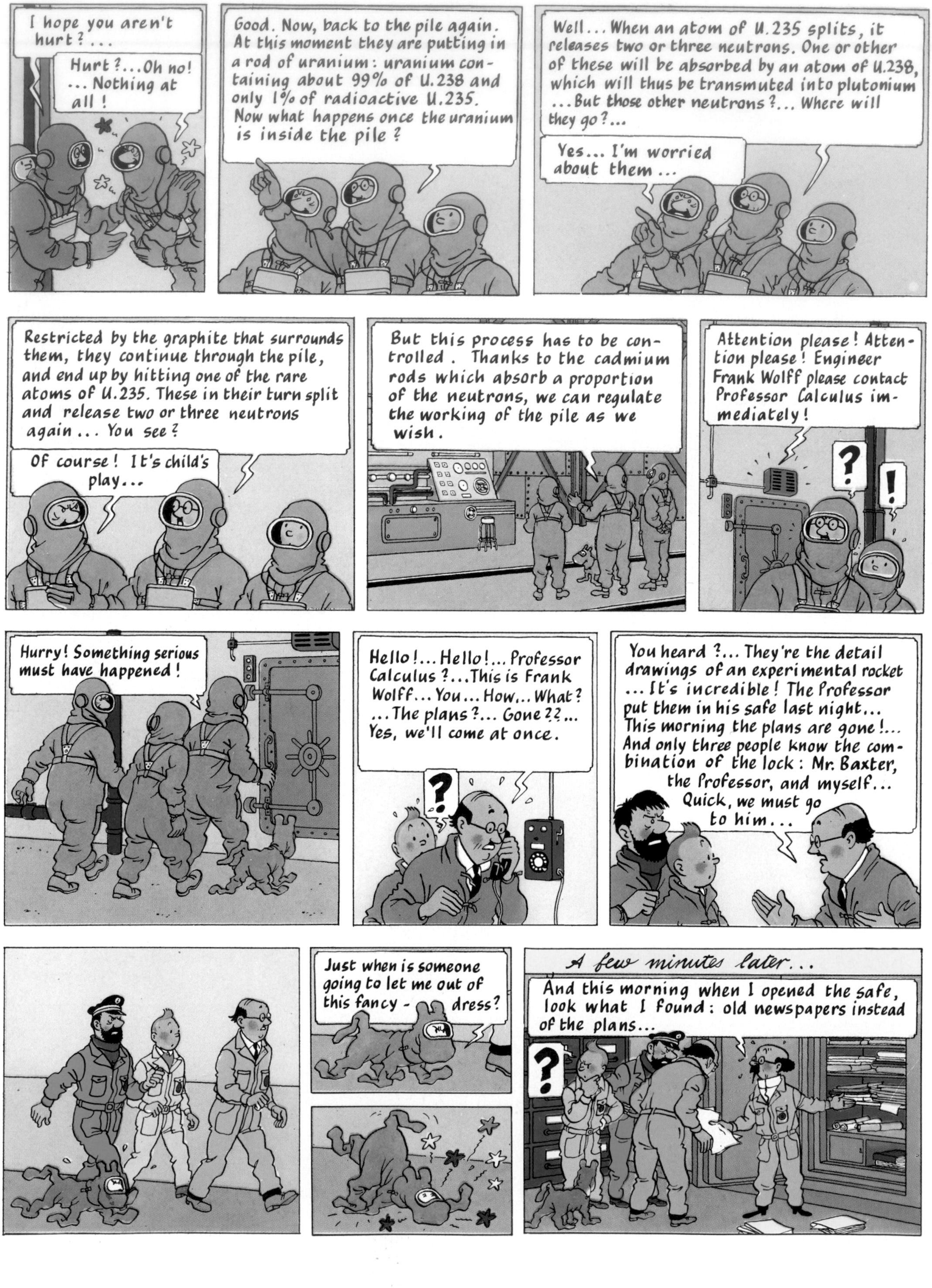

I hope you aren't hurt? ...
Hurt?...Oh no! ... Nothing at all!
Good. Now, back to the pile again. At this moment they are putting in a rod of uranium: uranium containing about 99% of U.238 and only 1% of radioactive U.235. Now what happens once the uranium is inside the pile?
Well... When an atom of U.235 splits, it releases two or three neutrons. One or other of these will be absorbed by an atom of U.238, which will thus be transmuted into plutonium ...But those other neutrons?... Where will they go?...
Yes... I'm worried about them...
Restricted by the graphite that surrounds them, they continue through the pile, and end up by hitting one of the rare atoms of U.235. These in their turn split and release two or three neutrons again... You see?
Of course! It's child's play...
But this process has to be controlled. Thanks to the cadmium rods which absorb a proportion of the neutrons, we can regulate the working of the pile as we wish.
Attention please! Attention please! Engineer Frank Wolff please contact Professor Calculus immediately!
?
!
Hurry! Something serious must have happened!
Hello!... Hello!... Professor Calculus?...This is Frank Wolff... You... How... What? ...The plans?... Gone??... Yes, we'll come at once.
?
You heard?... They're the detail drawings of an experimental rocket ...It's incredible! The Professor put them in his safe last night... This morning the plans are gone!... And only three people know the combination of the lock: Mr. Baxter, the Professor, and myself... Quick, we must go to him...
Just when is someone going to let me out of this fancy-dress?
A few minutes later...
And this morning when I opened the safe, look what I found: old newspapers instead of the plans...
?

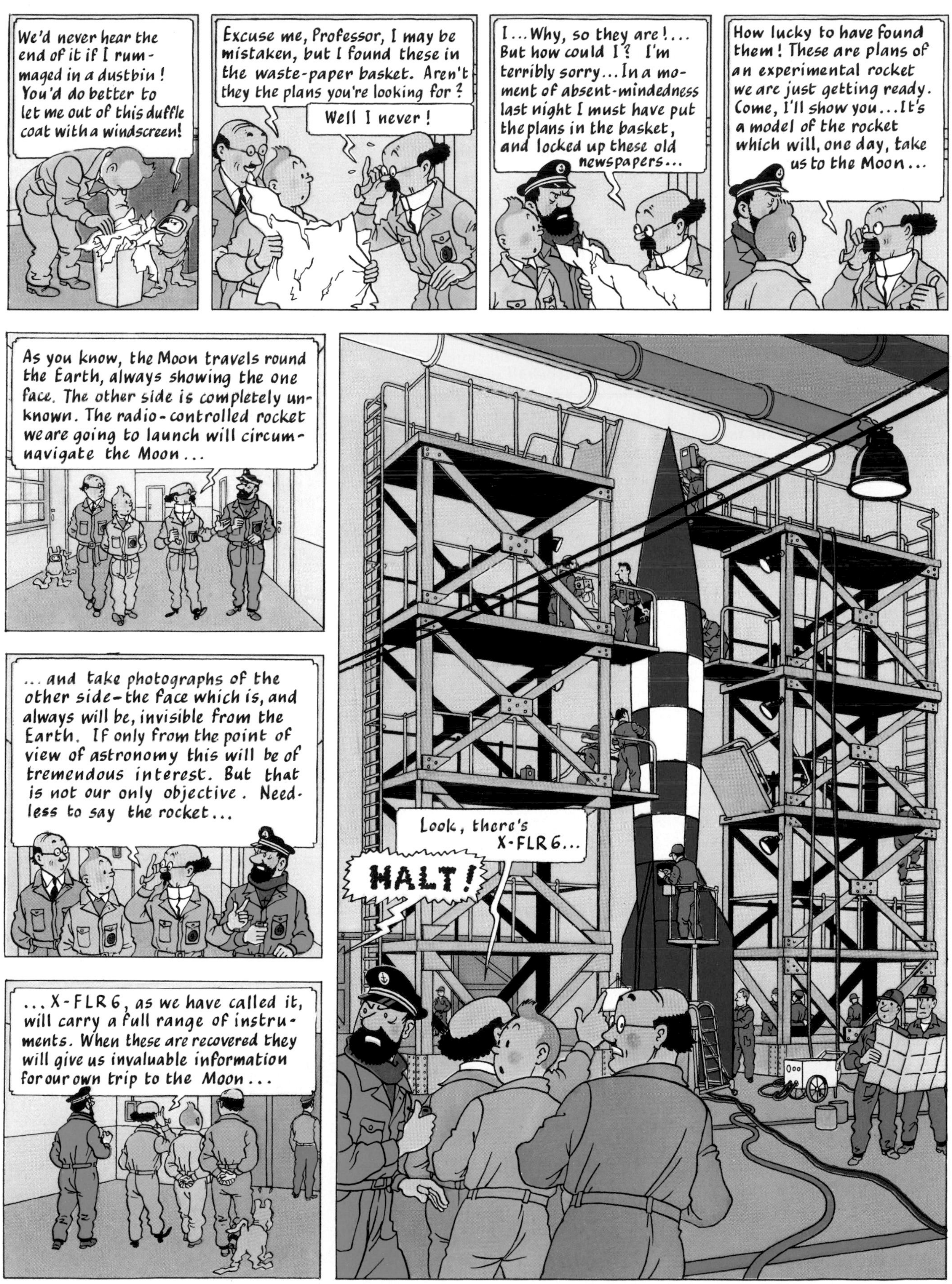
We'd never hear the end of it if I rummaged in a dustbin! You'd do better to let me out of this duffle coat with a windscreen!
Excuse me, Professor, I may be mistaken, but I found these in the waste-paper basket. Aren't they the plans you're looking for?
Well I never!
I... Why, so they are!... But how could I? I'm terribly sorry... In a moment of absent-mindedness last night I must have put the plans in the basket, and locked up these old newspapers...
How lucky to have found them! These are plans of an experimental rocket we are just getting ready. Come, I'll show you... It's a model of the rocket which will, one day, take us to the Moon...
As you know, the Moon travels round the Earth, always showing the one face. The other side is completely unknown. The radio-controlled rocket we are going to launch will circumnavigate the Moon...
... and take photographs of the other side - the face which is, and always will be, invisible from the Earth. If only from the point of view of astronomy this will be of tremendous interest. But that is not our only objective. Needless to say the rocket...
... X-FLR 6, as we have called it, will carry a full range of instruments. When these are recovered they will give us invaluable information for our own trip to the Moon...
HALT!
Look, there's X-FLR 6...

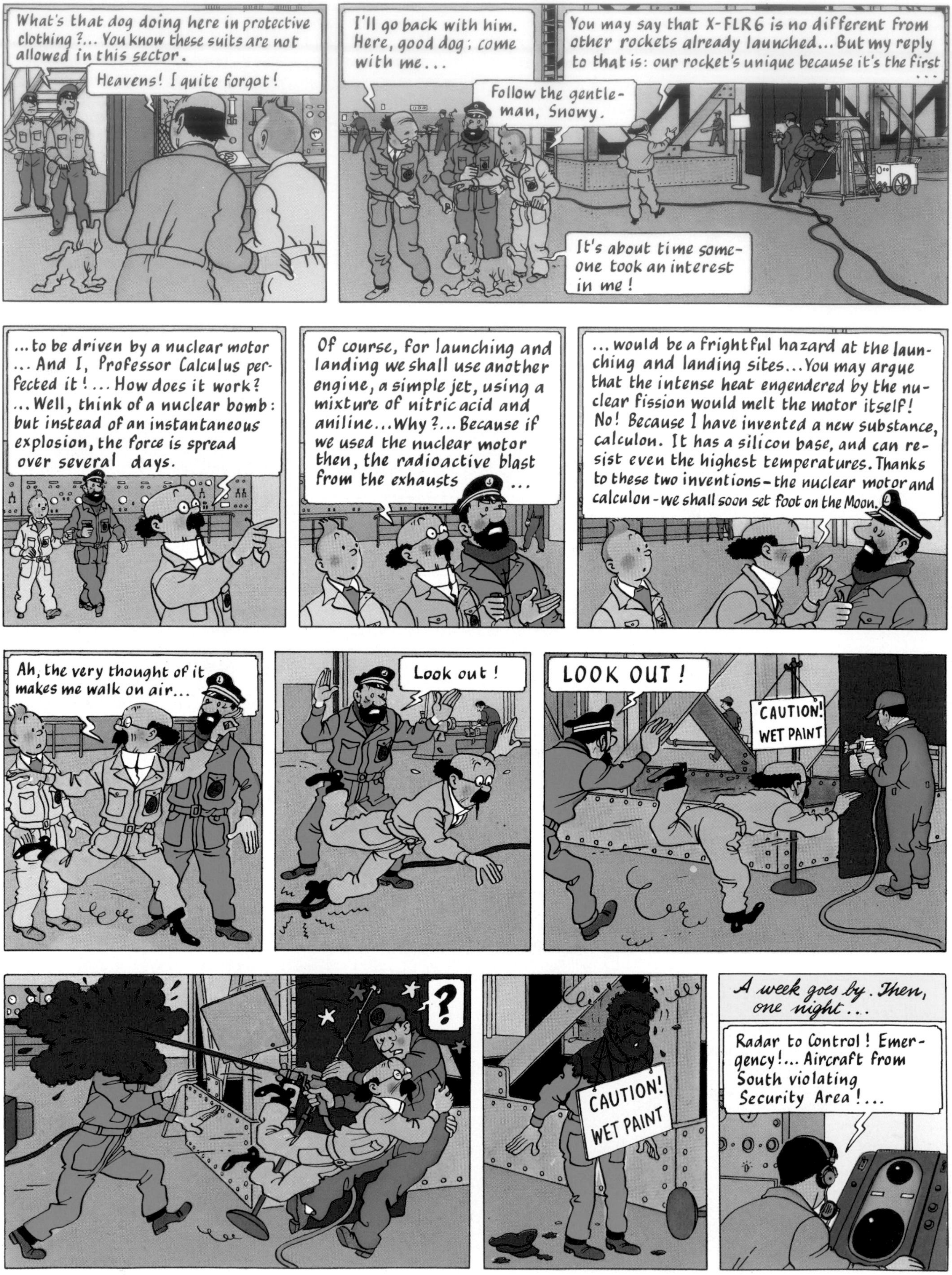
What's that dog doing here in protective clothing?... You know these suits are not allowed in this sector.
Heavens! I quite forgot!
I'll go back with him. Here, good dog; come with me...
You may say that X-FLR6 is no different from other rockets already launched... But my reply to that is: our rocket's unique because it's the first ...
Follow the gentleman, Snowy.
It's about time someone took an interest in me!
...to be driven by a nuclear motor ... And I, Professor Calculus perfected it!... How does it work? ...Well, think of a nuclear bomb: but instead of an instantaneous explosion, the force is spread over several days.
Of course, for launching and landing we shall use another engine, a simple jet, using a mixture of nitric acid and aniline... Why?... Because if we used the nuclear motor then, the radioactive blast from the exhausts ...
... would be a frightful hazard at the launching and landing sites... You may argue that the intense heat engendered by the nuclear fission would melt the motor itself! No! Because I have invented a new substance, calculon. It has a silicon base, and can resist even the highest temperatures. Thanks to these two inventions - the nuclear motor and calculon - we shall soon set foot on the Moon.
Ah, the very thought of it makes me walk on air...
Look out!
LOOK OUT!
CAUTION! WET PAINT
?
CAUTION! WET PAINT
A week goes by. Then, one night...
Radar to Control! Emergency!... Aircraft from South violating Security Area!...

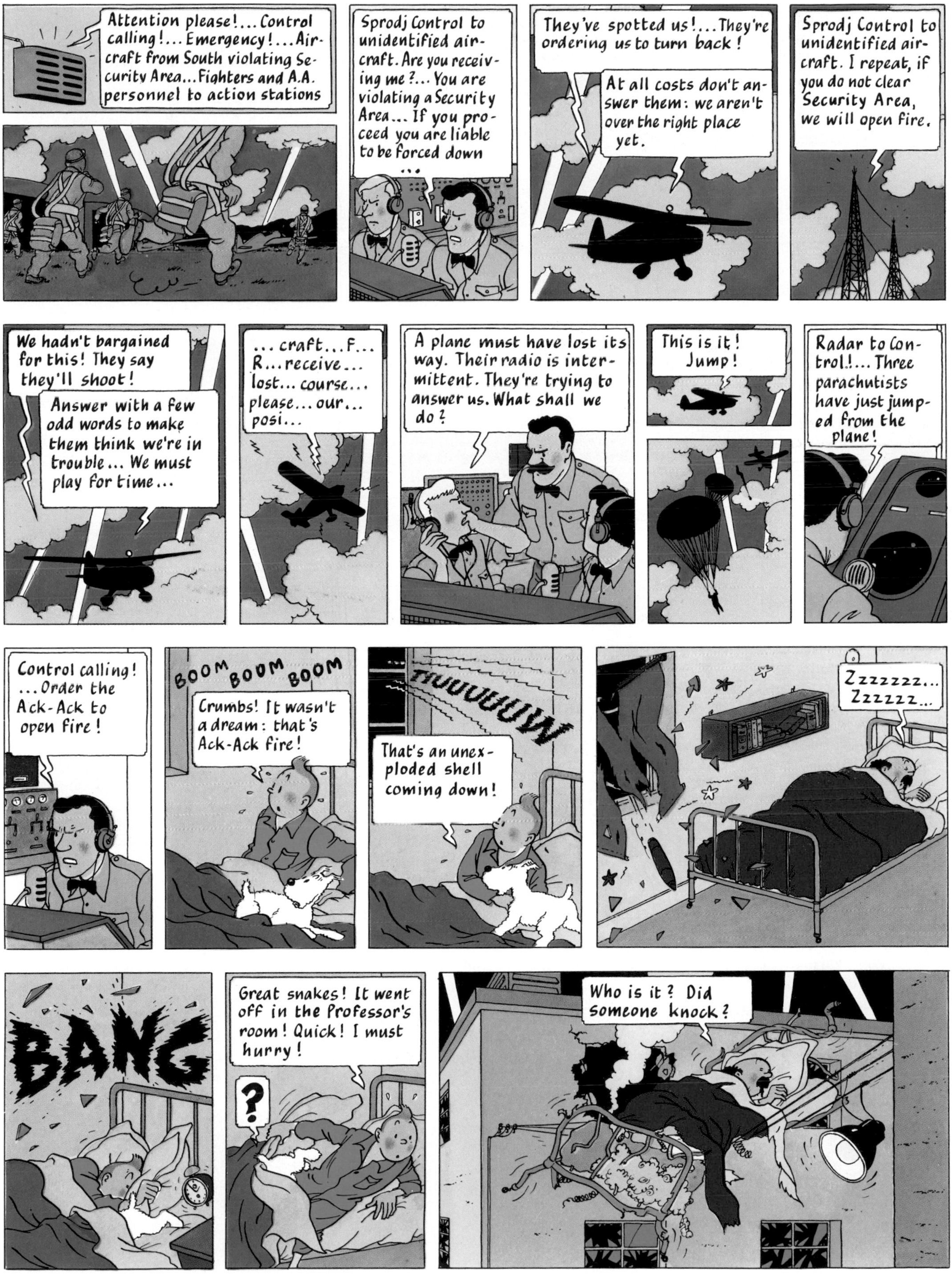
Attention please!... Control calling!... Emergency!... Aircraft from South violating Security Area... Fighters and A.A. personnel to action stations
Sprodj Control to unidentified aircraft. Are you receiving me?... You are violating a Security Area... If you proceed you are liable to be forced down ...
They've spotted us!... They're ordering us to turn back!
At all costs don't answer them: we aren't over the right place yet.
Sprodj Control to unidentified aircraft. I repeat, if you do not clear Security Area, we will open fire.
We hadn't bargained for this! They say they'll shoot!
Answer with a few odd words to make them think we're in trouble... We must play for time...
... craft... F... R... receive... lost... course... please... our... posi...
A plane must have lost its way. Their radio is intermittent. They're trying to answer us. What shall we do?
This is it! Jump!
Radar to Control!... Three parachutists have just jumped from the plane!
Control calling! ... Order the Ack-Ack to open fire!
BOOM BOOM BOOM
Crumbs! It wasn't a dream: that's Ack-Ack fire!
TIUUUUUUW
That's an unexploded shell coming down!
Zzzzzzz... Zzzzzz...
BANG
Great snakes! It went off in the Professor's room! Quick! I must hurry!
?
Who is it? Did someone knock?

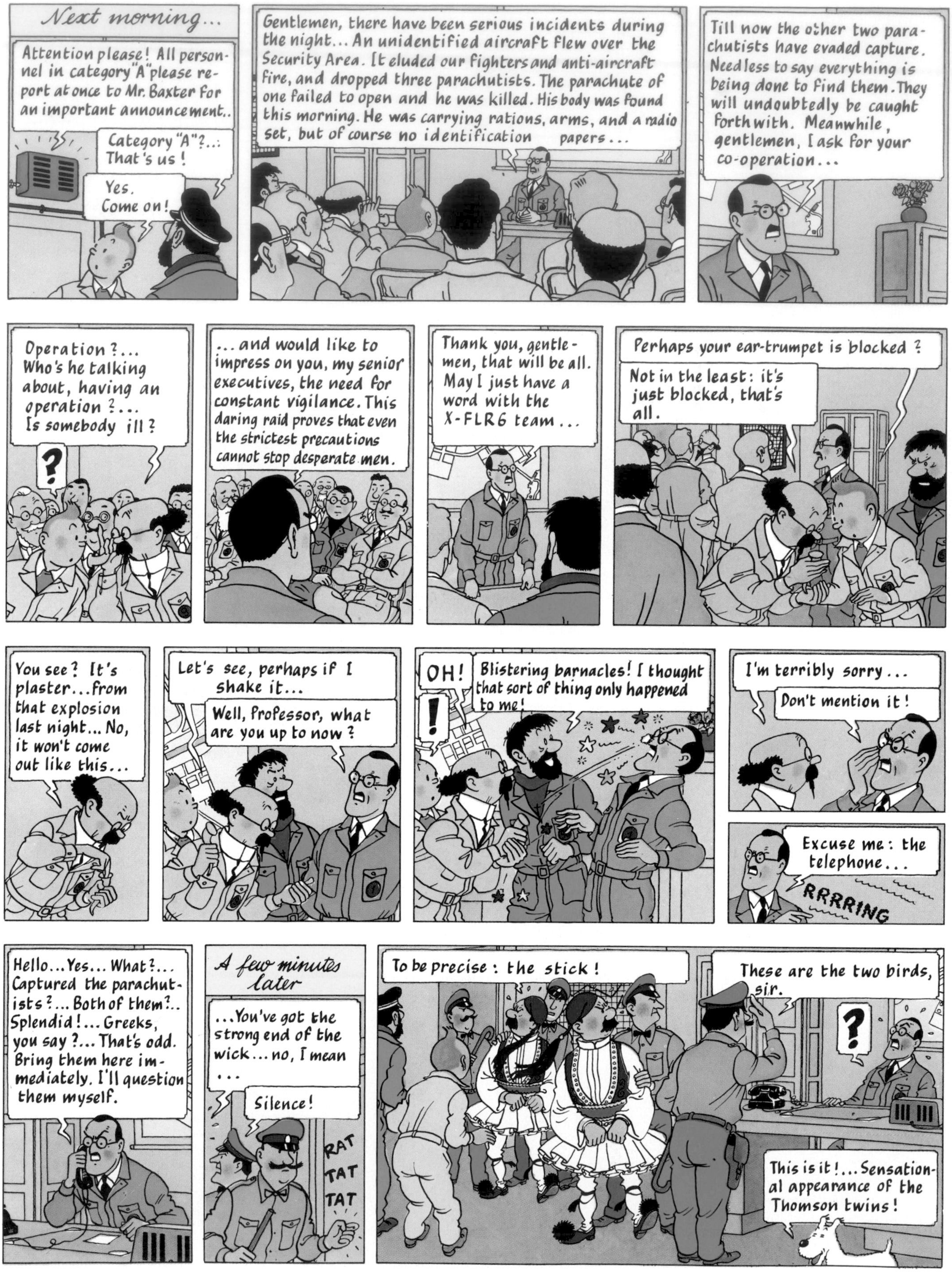

Next morning...
Attention please! All personnel in category "A" please report at once to Mr. Baxter for an important announcement..
Category "A"?... That's us!
Yes. Come on!
Gentlemen, there have been serious incidents during the night... An unidentified aircraft flew over the Security Area. It eluded our fighters and anti-aircraft fire, and dropped three parachutists. The parachute of one failed to open and he was killed. His body was found this morning. He was carrying rations, arms, and a radio set, but of course no identification papers...
Till now the other two parachutists have evaded capture. Needless to say everything is being done to find them. They will undoubtedly be caught forthwith. Meanwhile, gentlemen, I ask for your co-operation...
Operation?... Who's he talking about, having an operation?... Is somebody ill?
?
...and would like to impress on you, my senior executives, the need for constant vigilance. This daring raid proves that even the strictest precautions cannot stop desperate men.
Thank you, gentlemen, that will be all. May I just have a word with the X-FLR6 team...
Perhaps your ear-trumpet is blocked?
Not in the least: it's just blocked, that's all.
You see? It's plaster... from that explosion last night... No, it won't come out like this...
Let's see, perhaps if I shake it...
Well, Professor, what are you up to now?
OH!
!
Blistering barnacles! I thought that sort of thing only happened to me!
I'm terribly sorry...
Don't mention it!
Excuse me: the telephone...
RRRRING
Hello... Yes... What?... Captured the parachutists?... Both of them?.. Splendid!... Greeks, you say?... That's odd. Bring them here immediately. I'll question them myself.
A few minutes later
...You've got the strong end of the wick... no, I mean ...
Silence!
RAT TAT TAT
To be precise: the stick!
These are the two birds, sir.
?
This is it!... Sensational appearance of the Thomson twins!

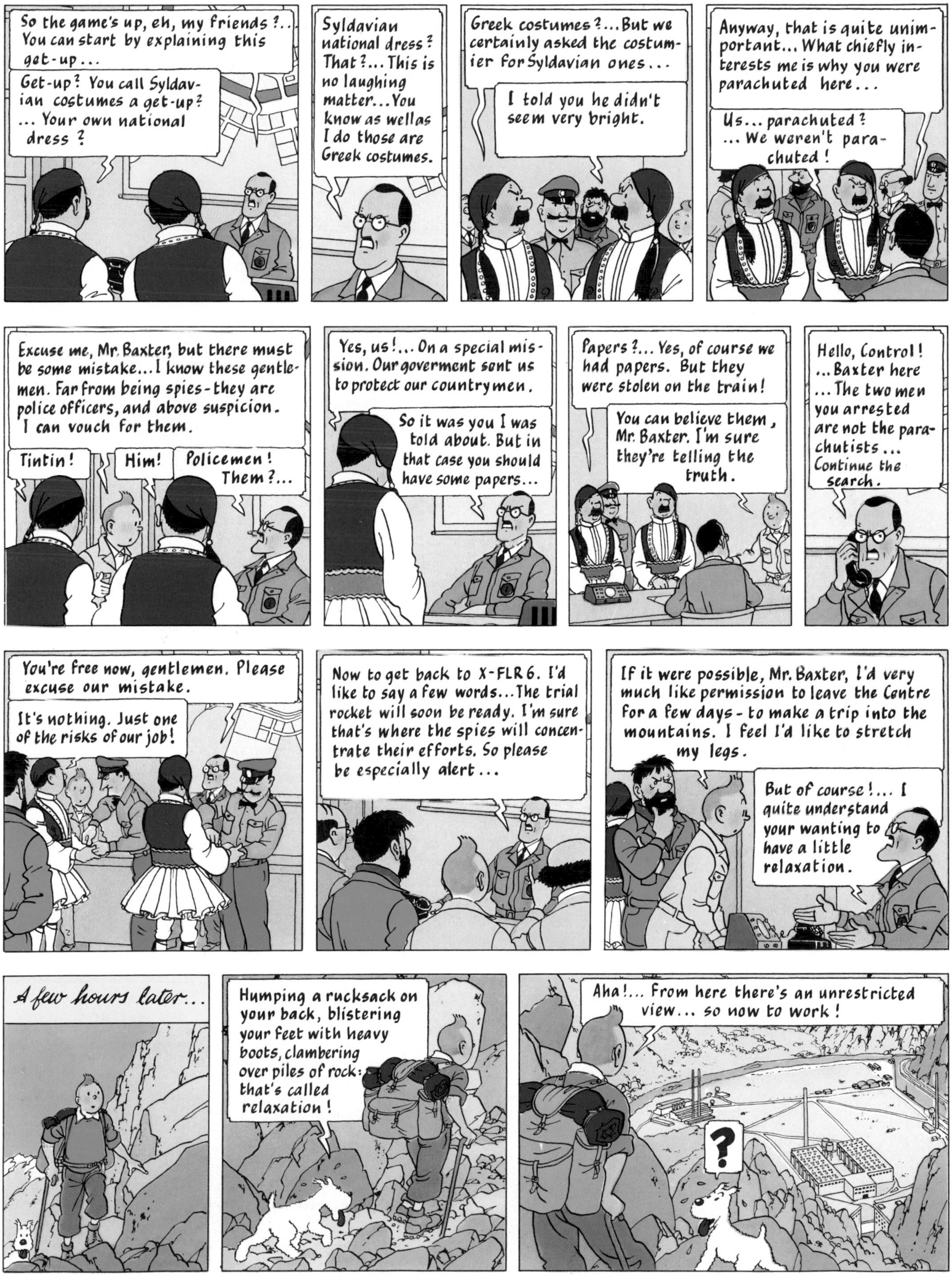
So the game's up, eh, my friends ?.. You can start by explaining this get-up...
Get-up? You call Syldavian costumes a get-up? ... Your own national dress ?
Syldavian national dress? That?... This is no laughing matter... You know as well as I do those are Greek costumes.
Greek costumes?... But we certainly asked the costumier for Syldavian ones...
I told you he didn't seem very bright.
Anyway, that is quite unimportant... What chiefly interests me is why you were parachuted here...
Us... parachuted? ... We weren't parachuted !
Excuse me, Mr. Baxter, but there must be some mistake... I know these gentlemen. Far from being spies - they are police officers, and above suspicion. I can vouch for them.
Tintin!
Him!
Policemen! Them?...
Yes, us!... On a special mission. Our goverment sent us to protect our countrymen.
So it was you I was told about. But in that case you should have some papers...
Papers?... Yes, of course we had papers. But they were stolen on the train!
You can believe them, Mr. Baxter. I'm sure they're telling the truth.
Hello, Control! ... Baxter here ... The two men you arrested are not the parachutists... Continue the search.
You're free now, gentlemen. Please excuse our mistake.
It's nothing. Just one of the risks of our job!
Now to get back to X-FLR 6. I'd like to say a few words... The trial rocket will soon be ready. I'm sure that's where the spies will concentrate their efforts. So please be especially alert...
If it were possible, Mr. Baxter, I'd very much like permission to leave the Centre for a few days - to make a trip into the mountains. I feel I'd like to stretch my legs.
But of course!... I quite understand your wanting to have a little relaxation.
A few hours later...
Humping a rucksack on your back, blistering your feet with heavy boots, clambering over piles of rock: that's called relaxation!
Aha!... From here there's an unrestricted view... so now to work!
?

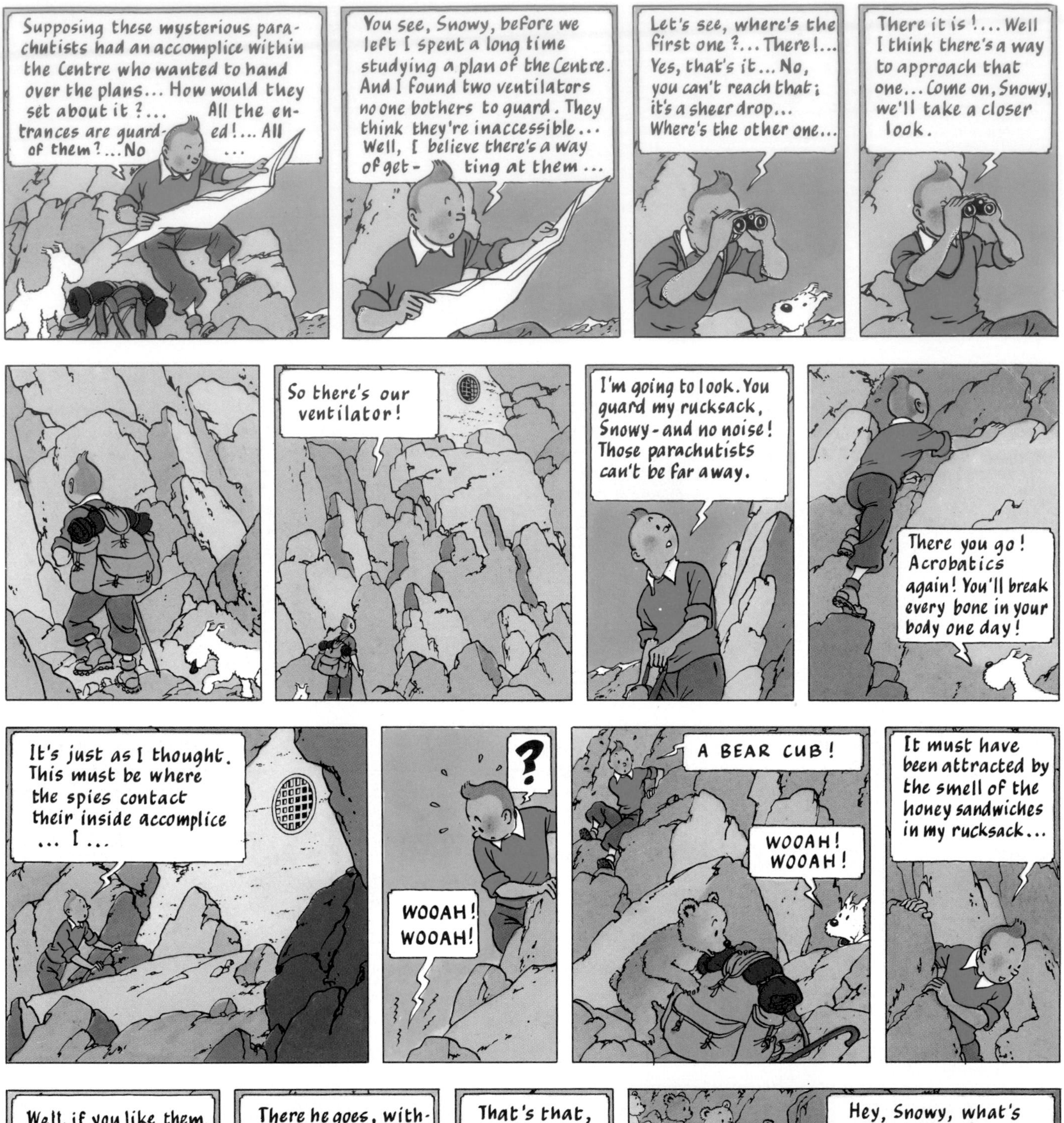
Supposing these mysterious parachutists had an accomplice within the Centre who wanted to hand over the plans... How would they set about it ?... All the entrances are guarded!... All of them?... No ...
You see, Snowy, before we left I spent a long time studying a plan of the Centre. And I found two ventilators no one bothers to guard. They think they're inaccessible... Well, I believe there's a way of getting at them...
Let's see, where's the first one ?... There!... Yes, that's it... No, you can't reach that; it's a sheer drop... Where's the other one...
There it is!... Well I think there's a way to approach that one... Come on, Snowy, we'll take a closer look.
So there's our ventilator!
I'm going to look. You guard my rucksack, Snowy - and no noise! Those parachutists can't be far away.
There you go! Acrobatics again! You'll break every bone in your body one day!
It's just as I thought. This must be where the spies contact their inside accomplice ... I ...
?
WOOAH! WOOAH!
A BEAR CUB!
WOOAH! WOOAH!
It must have been attracted by the smell of the honey sandwiches in my rucksack...
Well, if you like them, take one... Enjoy yourself, little greedy-guts!
There he goes, without waiting for more! ... And he didn't even say thank you!
That's that, eh, Snowy my boy? Here's a piece for you.
Hey, Snowy, what's the matter ?
!!

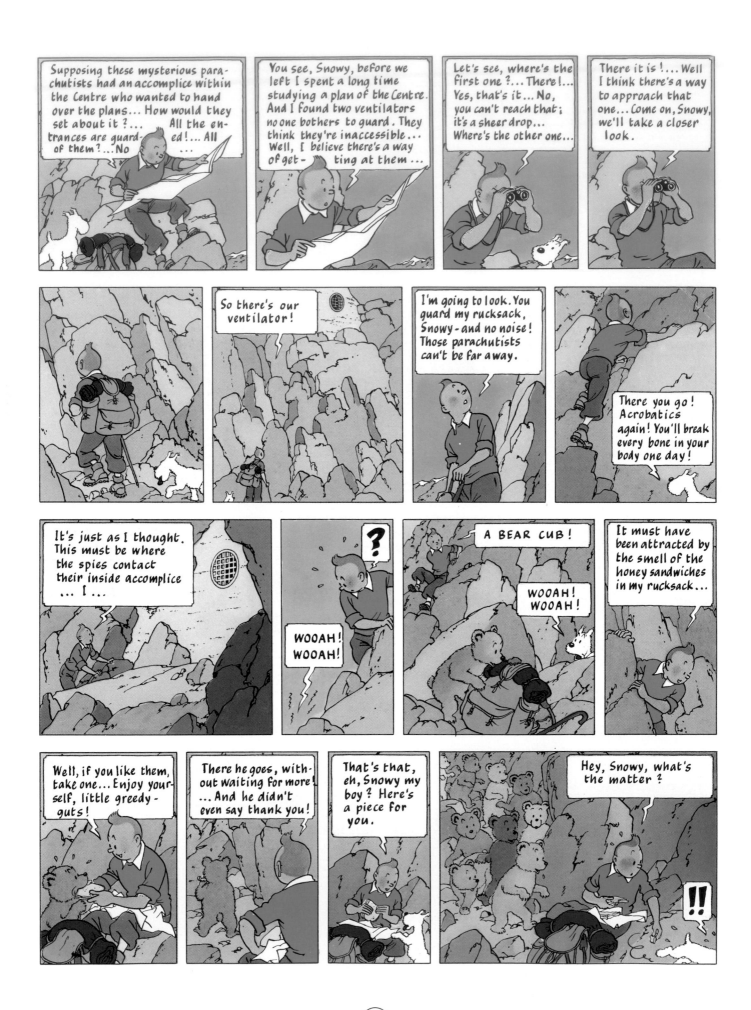

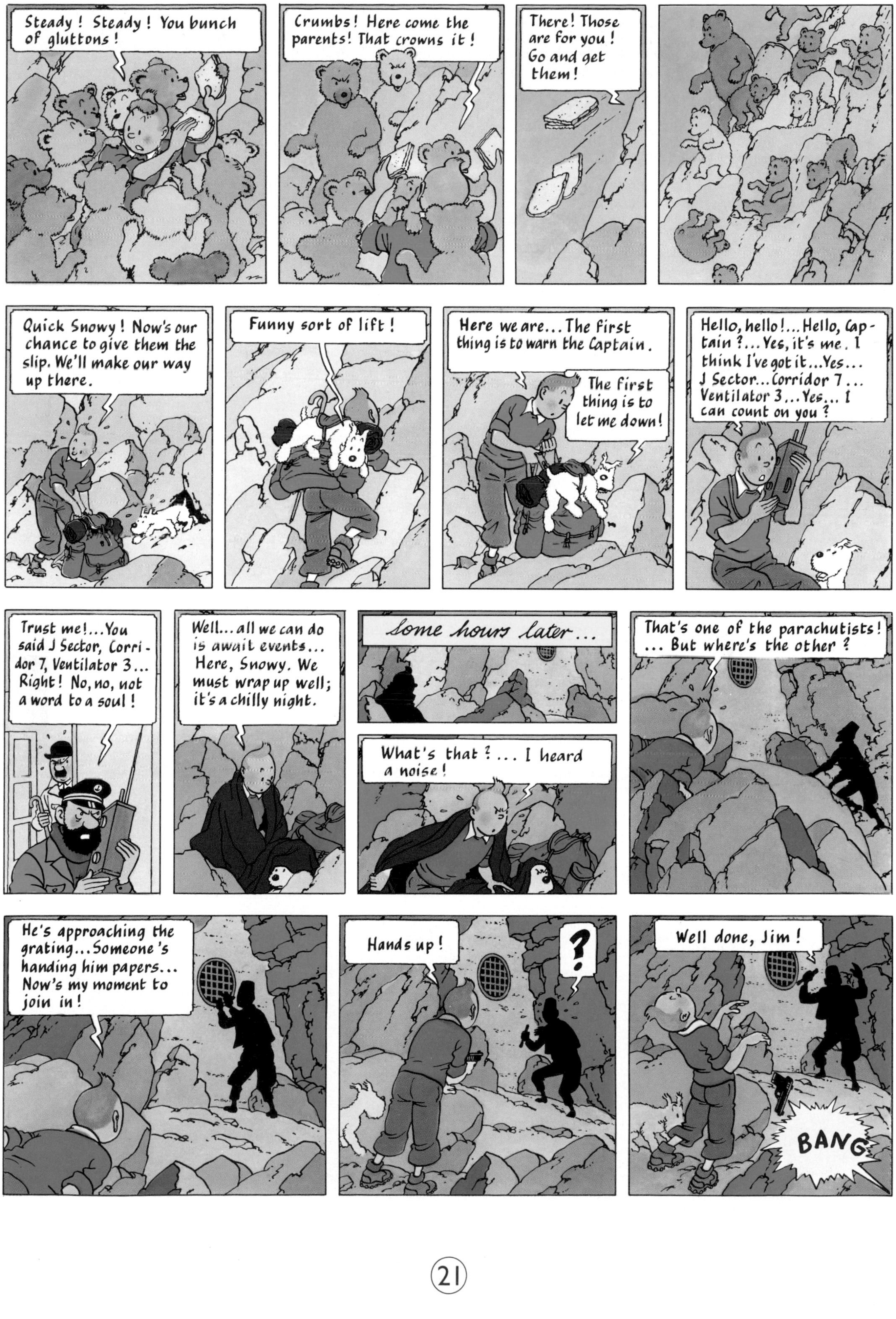
Steady! Steady! You bunch of gluttons!
Crumbs! Here come the parents! That crowns it!
There! Those are for you! Go and get them!
Quick Snowy! Now's our chance to give them the slip. We'll make our way up there.
Funny sort of lift!
Here we are... The first thing is to warn the Captain.
The first thing is to let me down!
Hello, hello!... Hello, Captain?... Yes, it's me. I think I've got it... Yes... J Sector... Corridor 7... Ventilator 3... Yes... I can count on you?
Trust me!... You said J Sector, Corridor 7, Ventilator 3... Right! No, no, not a word to a soul!
Well... all we can do is await events... Here, Snowy. We must wrap up well; it's a chilly night.
Some hours later...
What's that?... I heard a noise!
That's one of the parachutists! ... But where's the other?
He's approaching the grating... Someone's handing him papers... Now's my moment to join in!
Hands up!
?
Well done, Jim!
BANG

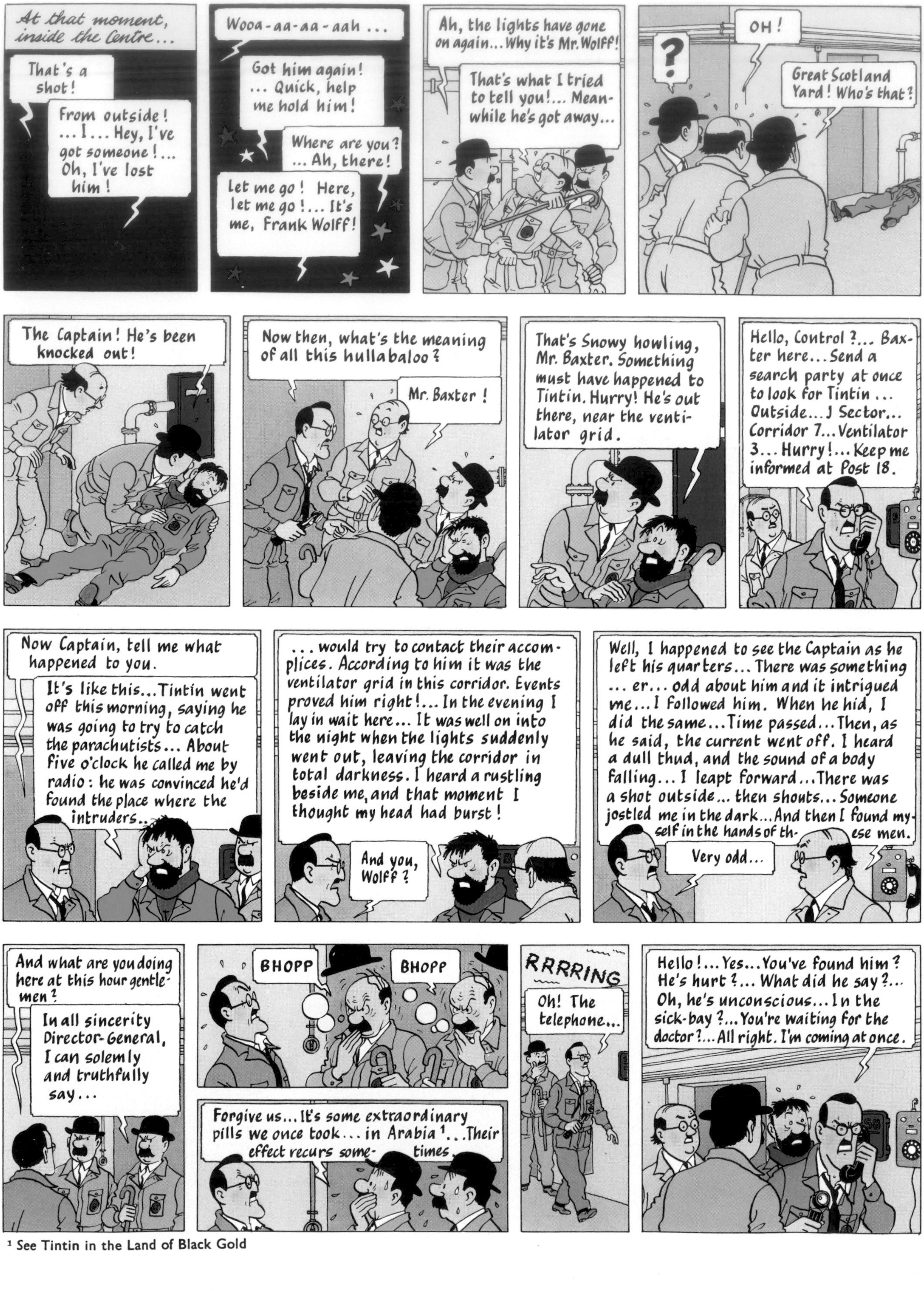
At that moment, inside the Centre...
That's a shot!
From outside! ... I... Hey, I've got someone!... Oh, I've lost him!
Wooa-aa-aa-aah ...
Got him again! ... Quick, help me hold him!
Where are you? ... Ah, there!
Let me go! Here, let me go!... It's me, Frank Wolff!
Ah, the lights have gone on again... Why it's Mr. Wolff!
That's what I tried to tell you!... Meanwhile he's got away...
OH!
?
Great Scotland Yard! Who's that?
The Captain! He's been knocked out!
Now then, what's the meaning of all this hullabaloo?
Mr. Baxter!
That's Snowy howling, Mr. Baxter. Something must have happened to Tintin. Hurry! He's out there, near the ventilator grid.
Hello, Control?... Baxter here... Send a search party at once to look for Tintin... Outside... J Sector... Corridor 7... Ventilator 3... Hurry!... Keep me informed at Post 18.
Now Captain, tell me what happened to you.
It's like this... Tintin went off this morning, saying he was going to try to catch the parachutists... About five o'clock he called me by radio: he was convinced he'd found the place where the intruders...
... would try to contact their accomplices. According to him it was the ventilator grid in this corridor. Events proved him right!... In the evening I lay in wait here... It was well on into the night when the lights suddenly went out, leaving the corridor in total darkness. I heard a rustling beside me, and that moment I thought my head had burst!
And you, Wolff?
Well, I happened to see the Captain as he left his quarters... There was something ... er... odd about him and it intrigued me... I followed him. When he hid, I did the same... Time passed... Then, as he said, the current went off. I heard a dull thud, and the sound of a body falling... I leapt forward... There was a shot outside... then shouts... Someone jostled me in the dark... And then I found myself in the hands of these men.
Very odd...
And what are you doing here at this hour gentlemen?
In all sincerity Director-General, I can solemly and truthfully say...
BHOPP
BHOPP
Forgive us... It's some extraordinary pills we once took... in Arabia¹... Their effect recurs sometimes.
RRRRING
Oh! The telephone...
Hello!... Yes... You've found him? He's hurt?... What did he say?... Oh, he's unconscious... In the sick-bay?... You're waiting for the doctor?... All right. I'm coming at once.

[1] See Tintin in the Land of Black Gold

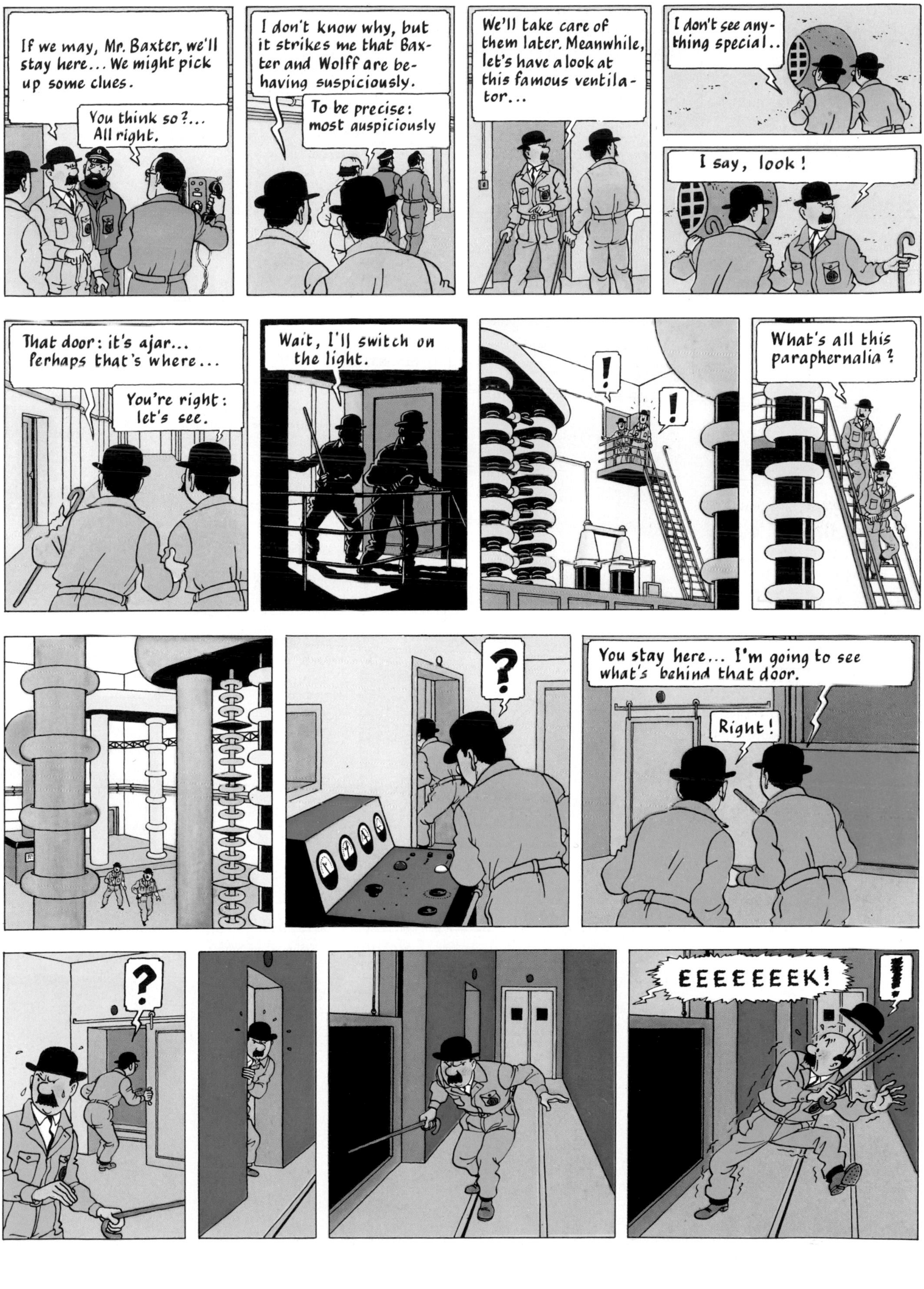
If we may, Mr. Baxter, we'll stay here... We might pick up some clues.
You think so?... All right.
I don't know why, but it strikes me that Baxter and Wolff are behaving suspiciously.
To be precise: most auspiciously
We'll take care of them later. Meanwhile, let's have a look at this famous ventilator...
I don't see anything special..
I say, look!
That door: it's ajar... Perhaps that's where...
You're right: let's see.
Wait, I'll switch on the light.
!
!
What's all this paraphernalia?
?
You stay here... I'm going to see what's behind that door.
Right!
?
EEEEEEEK!
!

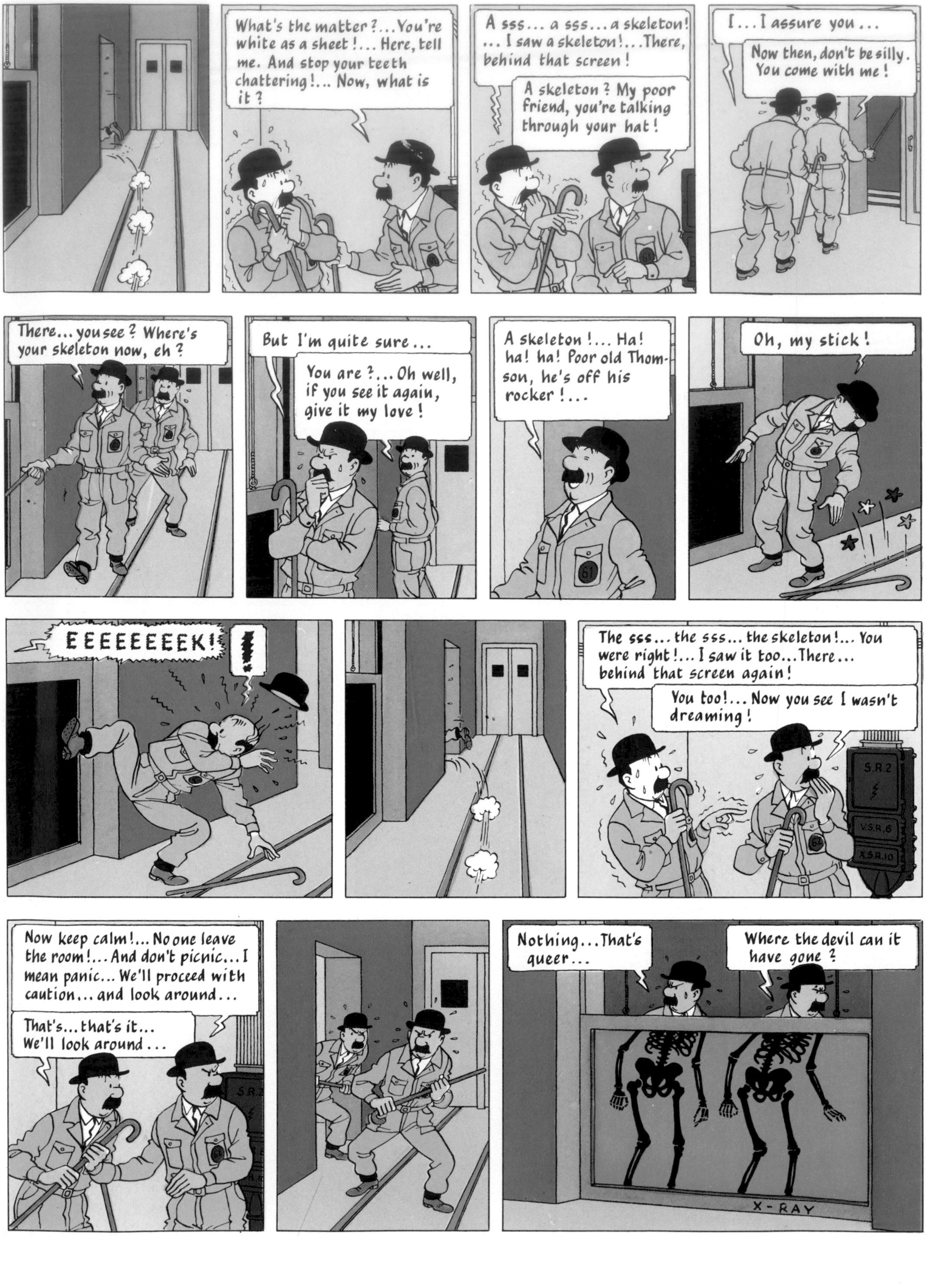
What's the matter ?... You're white as a sheet !... Here, tell me. And stop your teeth chattering !... Now, what is it ?
A sss... a sss... a skeleton ! ... I saw a skeleton !... There, behind that screen !
A skeleton ? My poor friend, you're talking through your hat !
I... I assure you...
Now then, don't be silly. You come with me !
There... you see ? Where's your skeleton now, eh ?
But I'm quite sure...
You are ?... Oh well, if you see it again, give it my love !
A skeleton !... Ha! ha! ha! Poor old Thomson, he's off his rocker !...
Oh, my stick !
EEEEEEEEK!
The sss... the sss... the skeleton !... You were right !... I saw it too... There... behind that screen again !
You too !... Now you see I wasn't dreaming !
S.R.2
V.S.R.6
X.S.R.10
Now keep calm !... No one leave the room !... And don't picnic... I mean panic... We'll proceed with caution... and look around...
That's... that's it... We'll look around...
Nothing... That's queer...
Where the devil can it have gone ?
X-RAY

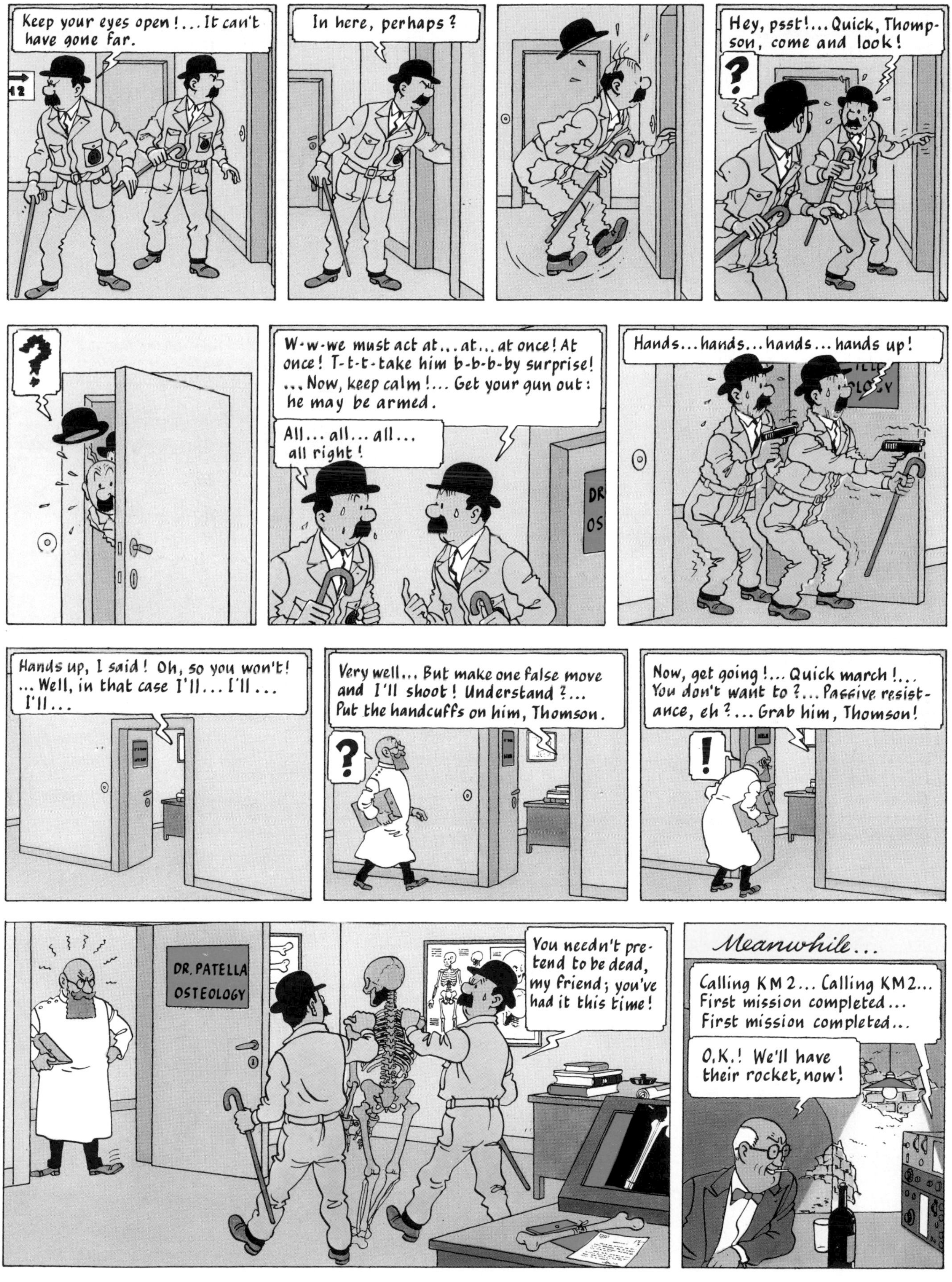
Keep your eyes open!... It can't have gone far.
In here, perhaps?
Hey, psst!... Quick, Thompson, come and look!
?
?
W-w-we must act at... at... at once! At once! T-t-t-take him b-b-b-by surprise! ... Now, keep calm!... Get your gun out: he may be armed.
All... all... all... all right!
Hands... hands... hands... hands up!
Hands up, I said! Oh, so you won't! ... Well, in that case I'll... I'll... I'll...
?
Very well... But make one false move and I'll shoot! Understand?... Put the handcuffs on him, Thomson.
!
Now, get going!... Quick march!... You don't want to?... Passive resistance, eh?... Grab him, Thomson!
DR. PATELLA OSTEOLOGY
You needn't pretend to be dead, my friend; you've had it this time!
Meanwhile...
Calling KM 2... Calling KM 2... First mission completed... First mission completed...
O.K.! We'll have their rocket, now!

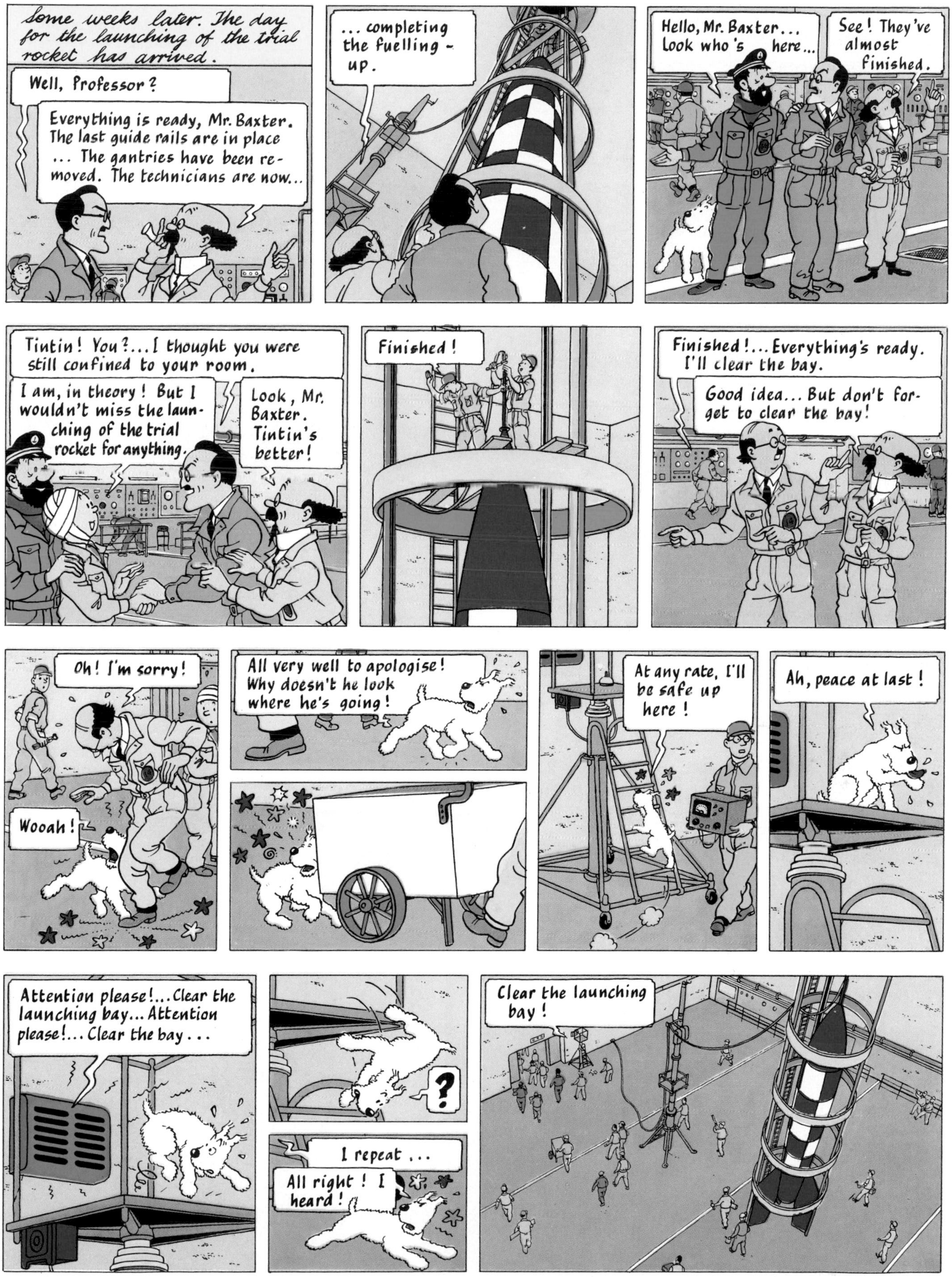
Some weeks later. The day for the launching of the trial rocket has arrived.
Well, Professor?
Everything is ready, Mr. Baxter. The last guide rails are in place ... The gantries have been removed. The technicians are now...
... completing the fuelling-up.
Hello, Mr. Baxter... Look who's here...
See! They've almost finished.
Tintin! You?... I thought you were still confined to your room.
I am, in theory! But I wouldn't miss the launching of the trial rocket for anything.
Look, Mr. Baxter. Tintin's better!
Finished!
Finished!... Everything's ready. I'll clear the bay.
Good idea... But don't forget to clear the bay!
Oh! I'm sorry!
Wooah!
All very well to apologise! Why doesn't he look where he's going!
At any rate, I'll be safe up here!
Ah, peace at last!
Attention please!... Clear the launching bay... Attention please!... Clear the bay...
?
I repeat...
All right! I heard!
Clear the launching bay!

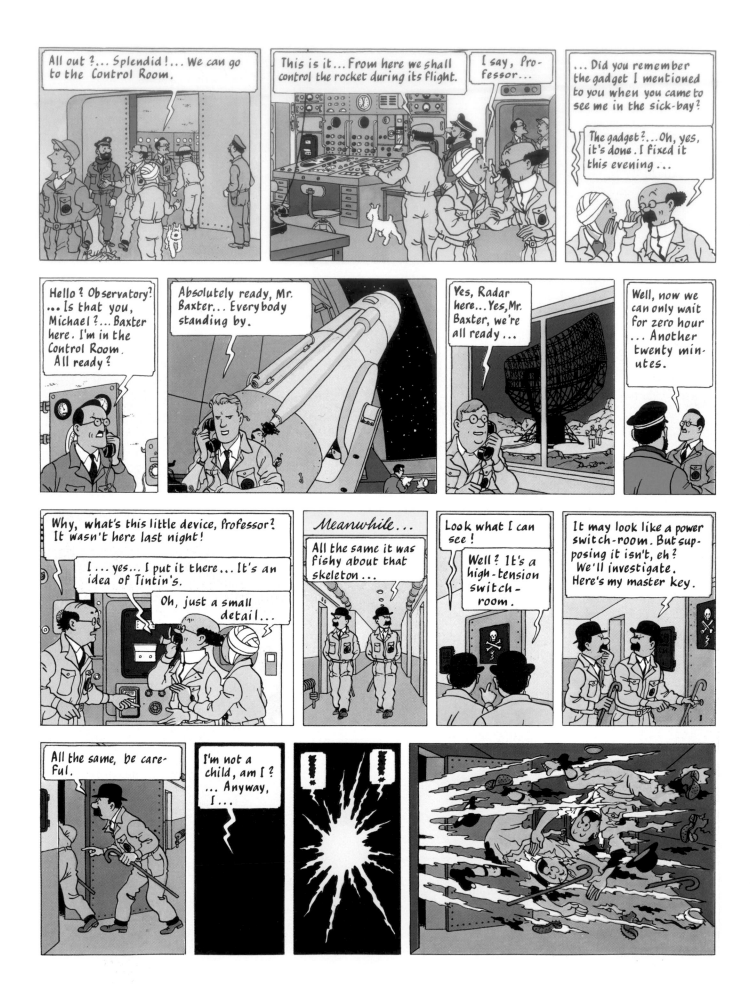

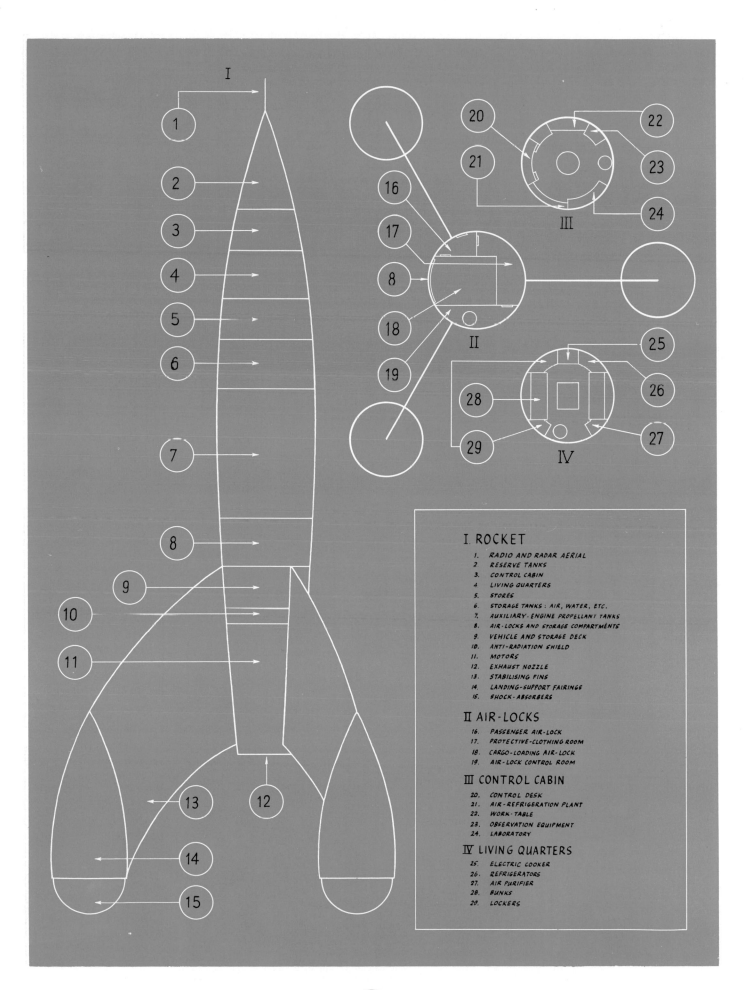

I. ROCKET

1. RADIO AND RADAR AERIAL
2. RESERVE TANKS
3. CONTROL CABIN
4. LIVING QUARTERS
5. STORES
6. STORAGE TANKS : AIR, WATER, ETC.
7. AUXILIARY-ENGINE PROPELLANT TANKS
8. AIR-LOCKS AND STORAGE COMPARTMENTS
9. VEHICLE AND STORAGE DECK
10. ANTI-RADIATION SHIELD
11. MOTORS
12. EXHAUST NOZZLE
13. STABILISING FINS
14. LANDING-SUPPORT FAIRINGS
15. SHOCK-ABSORBERS

II AIR-LOCKS

16. PASSENGER AIR-LOCK
17. PROTECTIVE-CLOTHING ROOM
18. CARGO-LOADING AIR-LOCK
19. AIR-LOCK CONTROL ROOM

III CONTROL CABIN

20. CONTROL DESK
21. AIR-REFRIGERATION PLANT
22. WORK-TABLE
23. OBSERVATION EQUIPMENT
24. LABORATORY

IV LIVING QUARTERS

25. ELECTRIC COOKER
26. REFRIGERATORS
27. AIR PURIFIER
28. BUNKS
29. LOCKERS

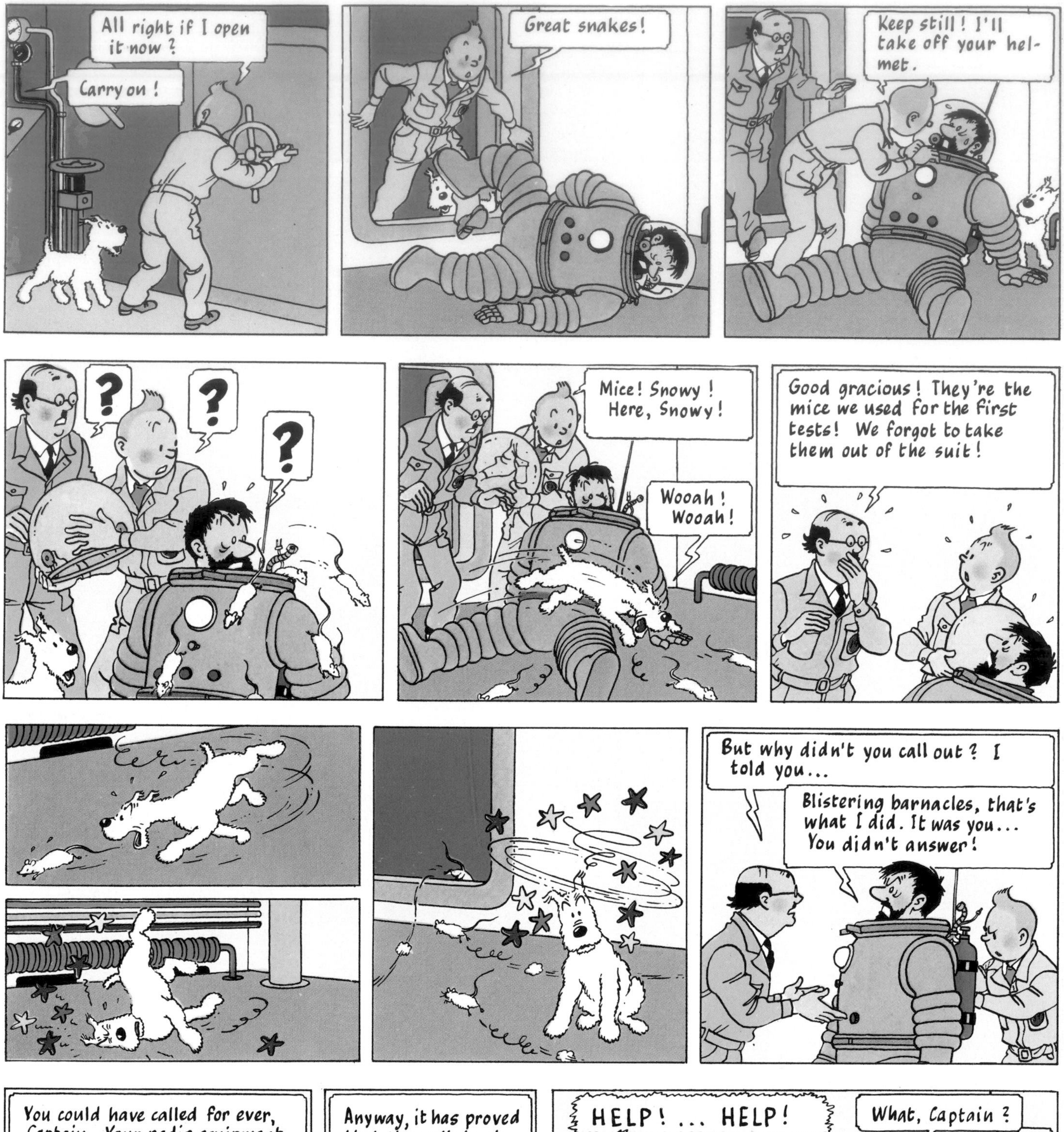
All right if I open it now ?
Carry on !
Great snakes !
Keep still ! I'll take off your helmet.
?
?
?
Mice ! Snowy ! Here, Snowy !
Wooah ! Wooah !
Good gracious ! They're the mice we used for the first tests ! We forgot to take them out of the suit !
But why didn't you call out ? I told you...
Blistering barnacles, that's what I did. It was you... You didn't answer !
You could have called for ever, Captain. Your radio equipment is disconnected !
Disconnected ! It'll be fun if that happens on the Moon !
Anyway, it has proved that the suit is absolutely resistant to a vacuum, and low temperatures... What happened was just a little incident... quite unimportant ...
HELP ! ... HELP !
What, Captain ?
?
?

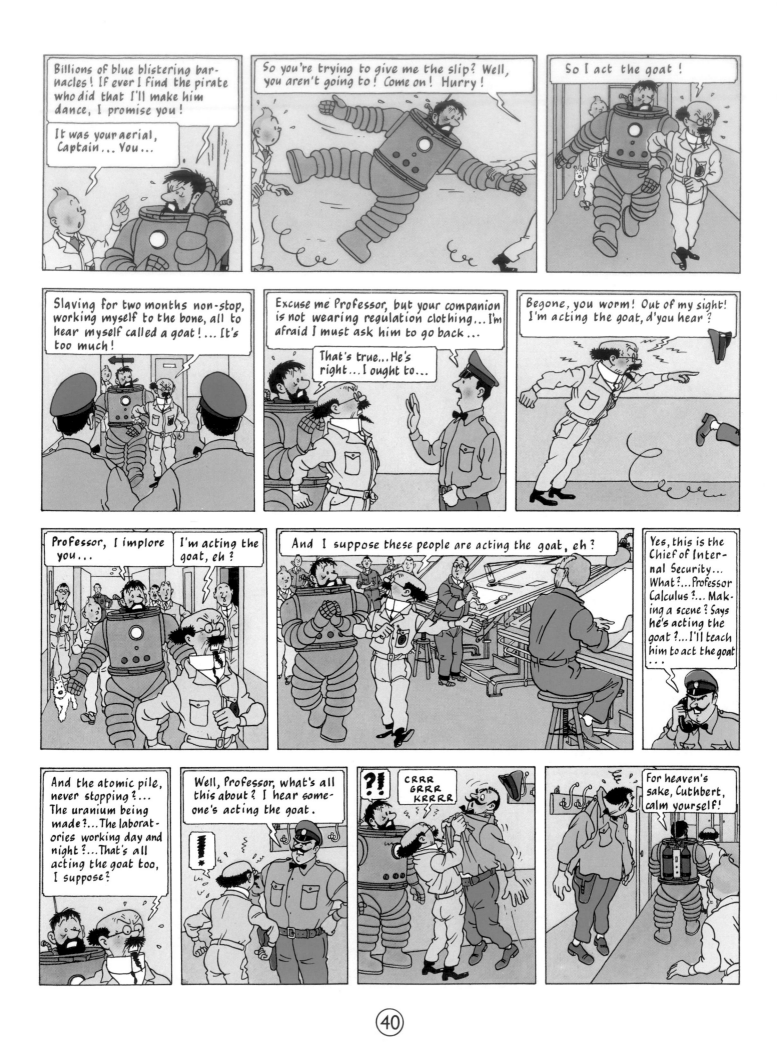

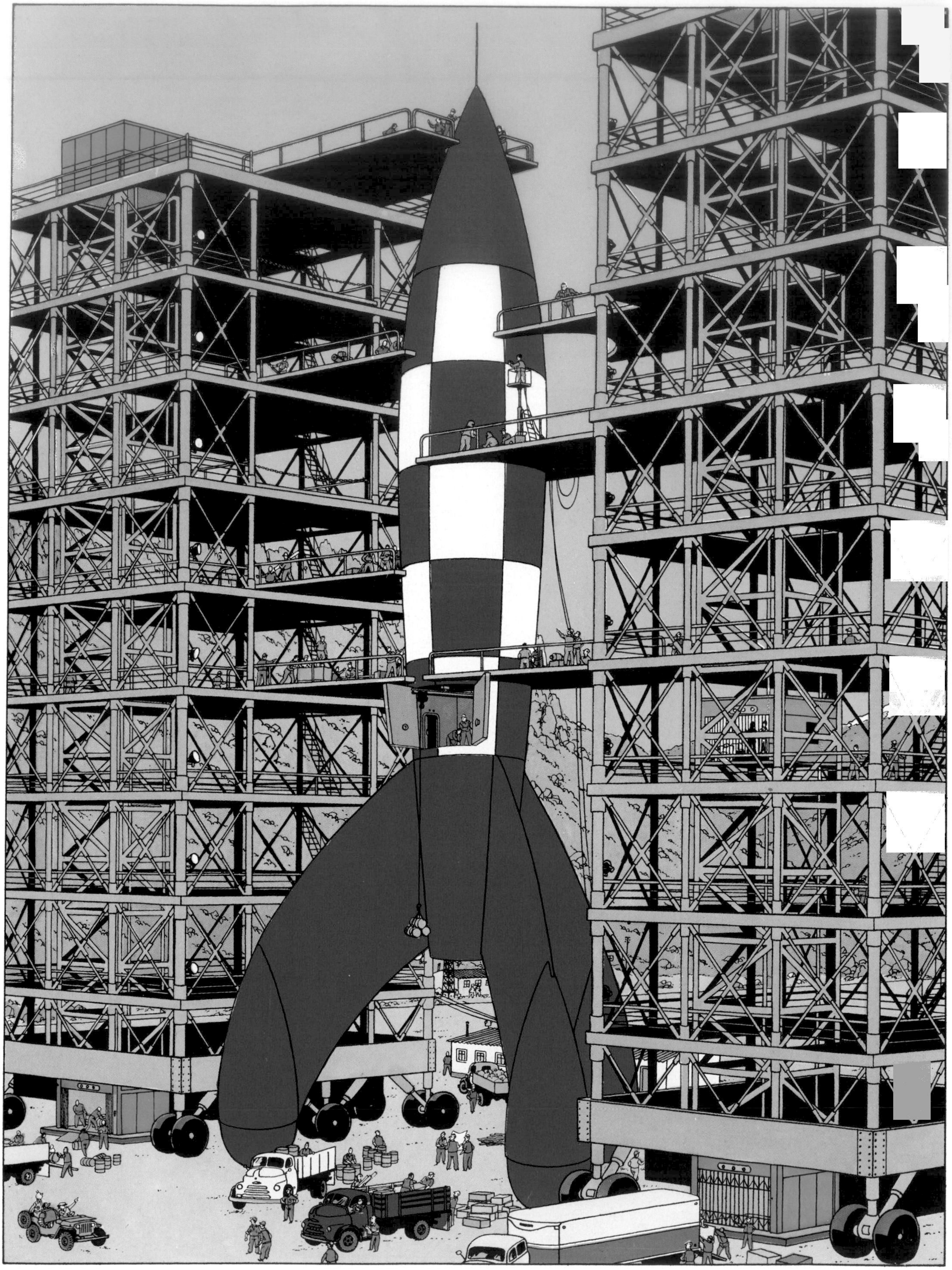

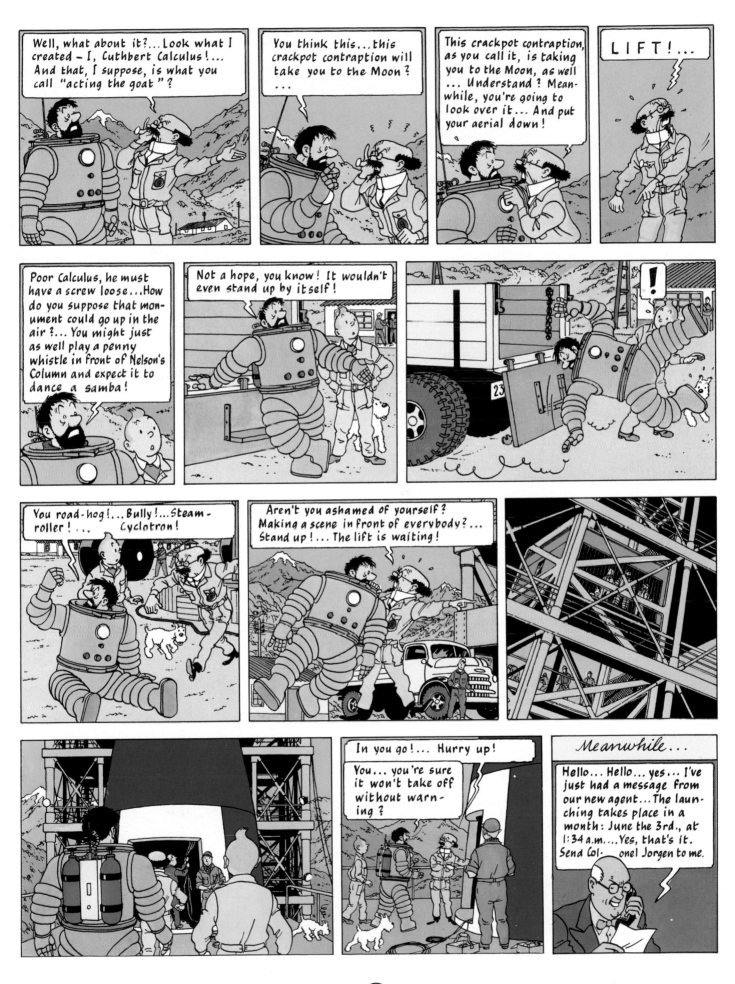

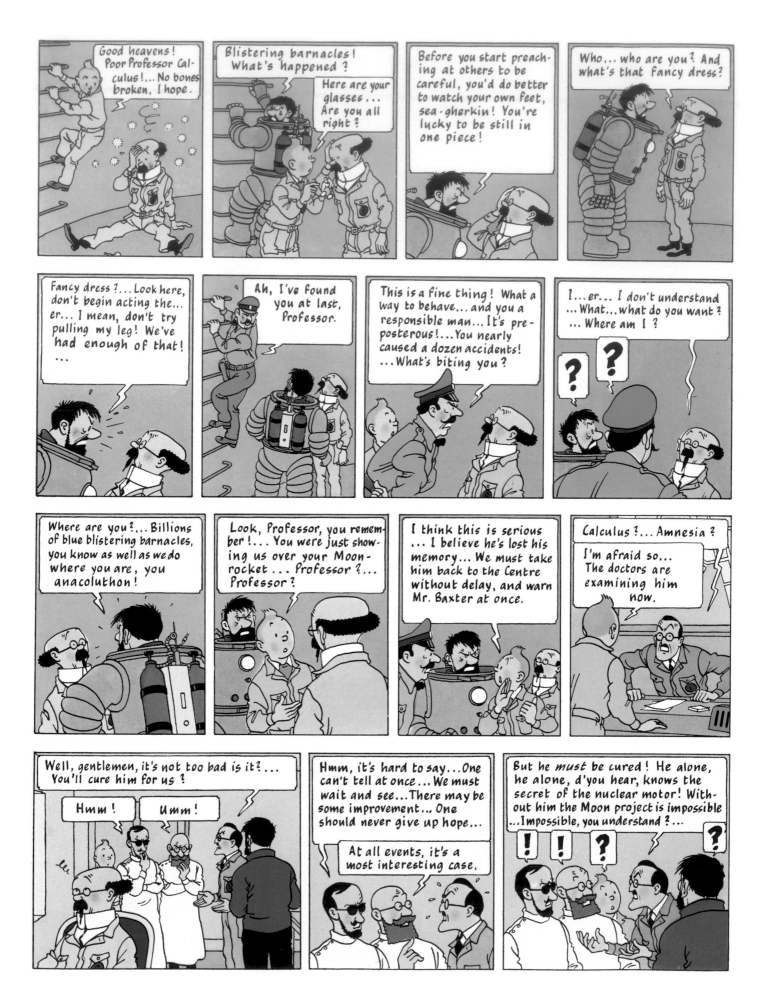

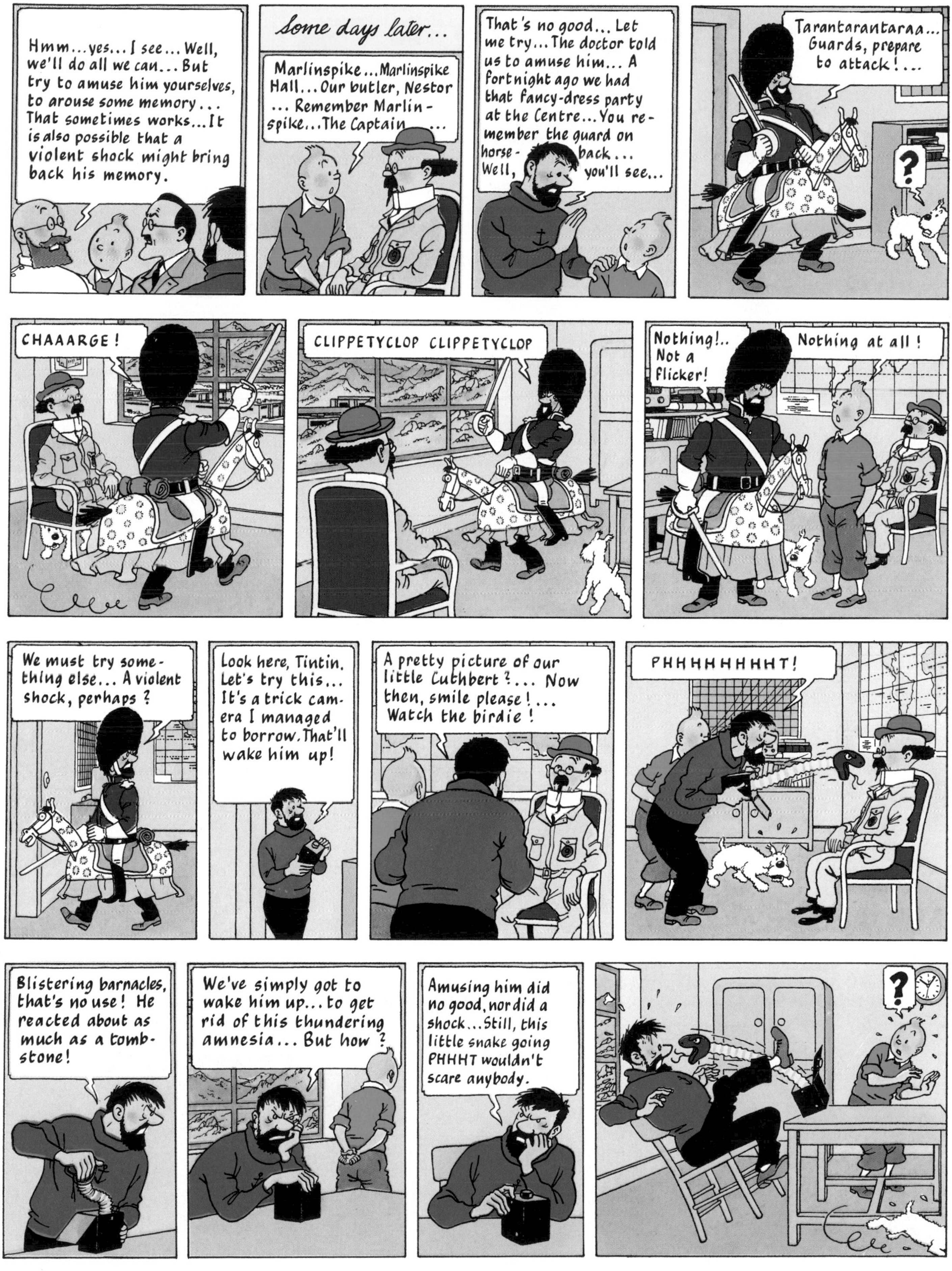
Hmm...yes...I see...Well, we'll do all we can...But try to amuse him yourselves, to arouse some memory... That sometimes works...It is also possible that a violent shock might bring back his memory.
Some days later...
Marlinspike...Marlinspike Hall...Our butler, Nestor ... Remember Marlin-spike...The Captain ...
That's no good... Let me try...The doctor told us to amuse him... A fortnight ago we had that fancy-dress party at the Centre...You remember the guard on horse-back... Well, you'll see...
Tarantarantaraa... Guards, prepare to attack!...
?
CHAAARGE!
CLIPPETYCLOP CLIPPETYCLOP
Nothing!.. Not a flicker!
Nothing at all!
We must try something else... A violent shock, perhaps?
Look here, Tintin. Let's try this... It's a trick camera I managed to borrow. That'll wake him up!
A pretty picture of our little Cuthbert?... Now then, smile please!... Watch the birdie!
PHHHHHHHHT!
Blistering barnacles, that's no use! He reacted about as much as a tombstone!
We've simply got to wake him up...to get rid of this thundering amnesia... But how?
Amusing him did no good, nor did a shock...Still, this little snake going PHHHT wouldn't scare anybody.
?

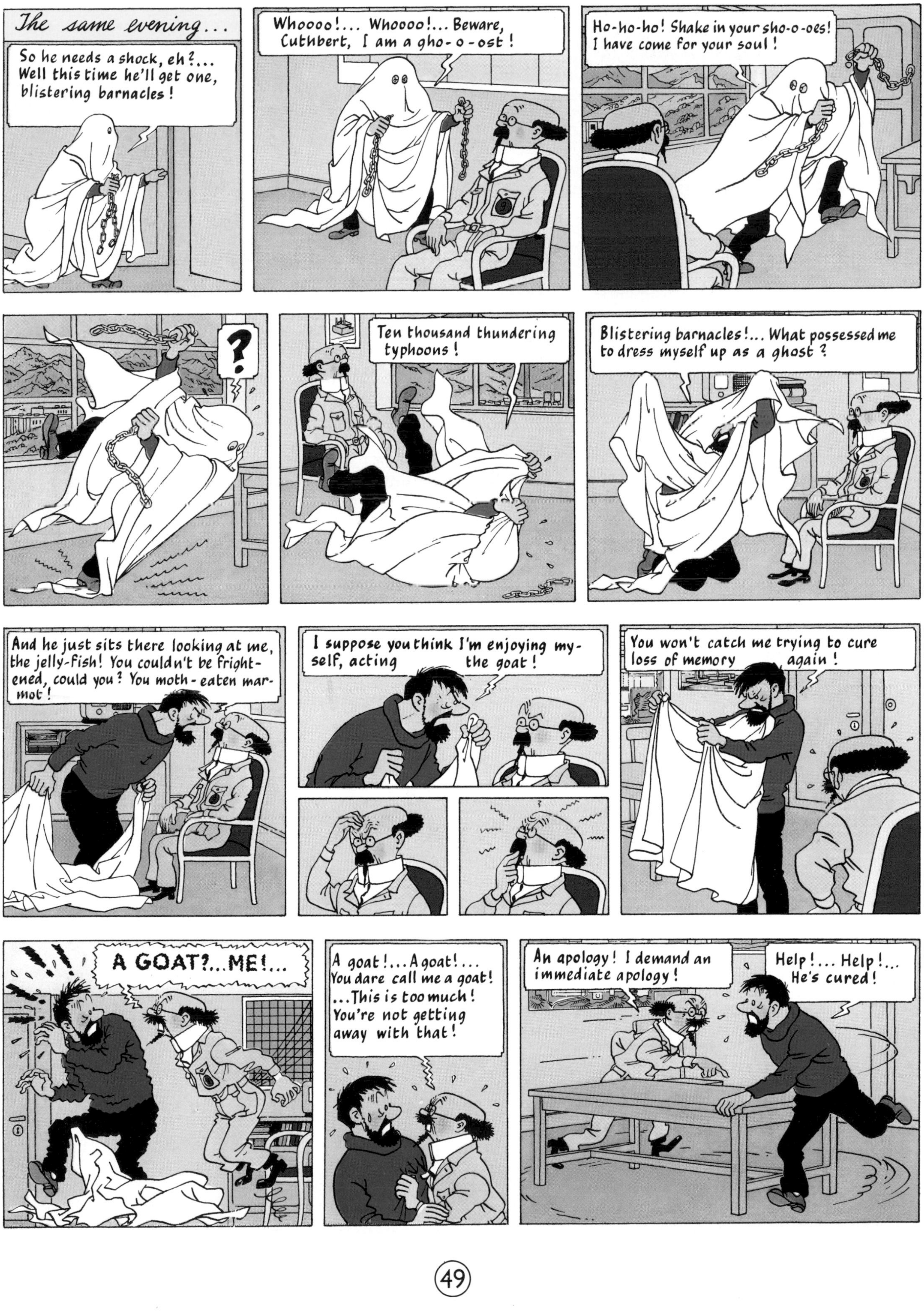
The same evening...
So he needs a shock, eh?... Well this time he'll get one, blistering barnacles!
Whoooo!... Whoooo!... Beware, Cuthbert, I am a gho-o-ost!
Ho-ho-ho! Shake in your sho-o-oes! I have come for your soul!
?
Ten thousand thundering typhoons!
Blistering barnacles!... What possessed me to dress myself up as a ghost?
And he just sits there looking at me, the jelly-fish! You couldn't be frightened, could you? You moth-eaten marmot!
I suppose you think I'm enjoying myself, acting the goat!
You won't catch me trying to cure loss of memory again!
A GOAT?...ME!...
A goat!... A goat!... You dare call me a goat! ...This is too much! You're not getting away with that!
An apology! I demand an immediate apology!
Help!... Help!... He's cured!

I must say you don't look very happy, Captain.

Why on earth should I look happy? Because we're off to the Moon?

To the Moon!... Don't make me laugh!... If that honky-tonk Calculus-machine doesn't blow up at the start, we'll find ourselves roaming around between the Great Bear and Jupiter, and never come back! You can hoot with laughter about that if you like!

No, I meant... Oh look, Captain! We're there!

Look! The gantries are flood-lit; the rocket is ready for launching! It's like magic!

Yes, very pretty... for the spectators! ...

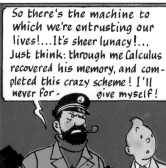

So there's the machine to which we're entrusting our lives!...It's sheer lunacy!... Just think: through me Calculus recovered his memory, and completed this crazy scheme! I'll never for-   give myself!

Meanwhile . . .

If there's no change of plan, it's just half an hour till their departure . . .

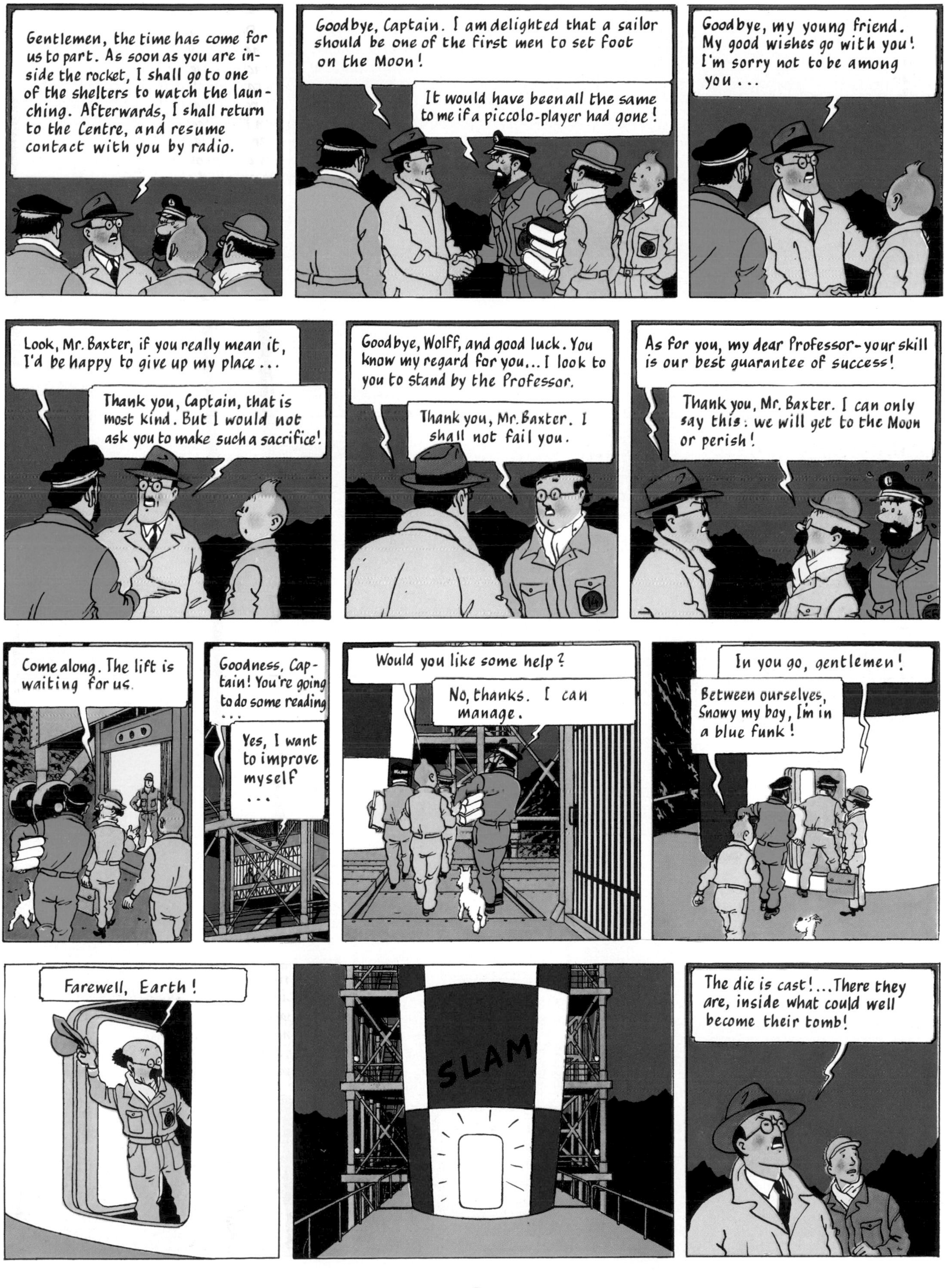
Gentlemen, the time has come for us to part. As soon as you are inside the rocket, I shall go to one of the shelters to watch the launching. Afterwards, I shall return to the Centre, and resume contact with you by radio.
Goodbye, Captain. I am delighted that a sailor should be one of the first men to set foot on the Moon!
It would have been all the same to me if a piccolo-player had gone!
Goodbye, my young friend. My good wishes go with you! I'm sorry not to be among you . . .
Look, Mr. Baxter, if you really mean it, I'd be happy to give up my place . . .
Thank you, Captain, that is most kind. But I would not ask you to make such a sacrifice!
Goodbye, Wolff, and good luck. You know my regard for you... I look to you to stand by the Professor.
Thank you, Mr. Baxter. I shall not fail you.
As for you, my dear Professor - your skill is our best guarantee of success!
Thank you, Mr. Baxter. I can only say this: we will get to the Moon or perish!
Come along. The lift is waiting for us.
Goodness, Captain! You're going to do some reading . . .
Yes, I want to improve myself . . .
Would you like some help?
No, thanks. I can manage.
In you go, gentlemen!
Between ourselves, Snowy my boy, I'm in a blue funk!
Farewell, Earth!
SLAM
The die is cast!...There they are, inside what could well become their tomb!

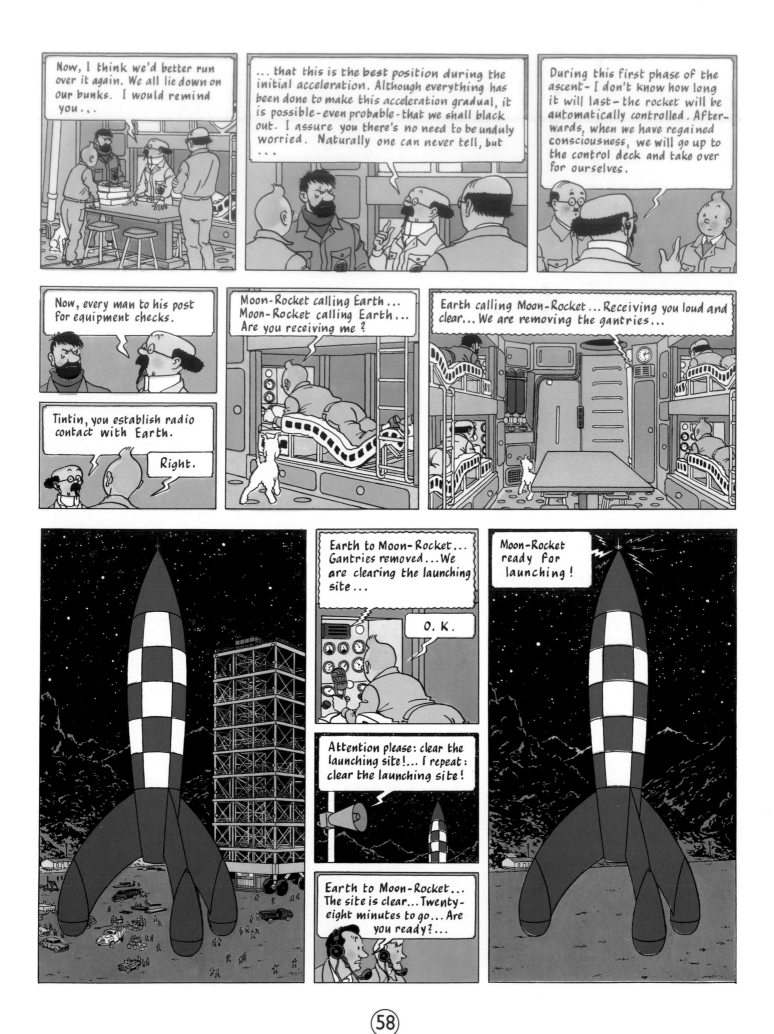

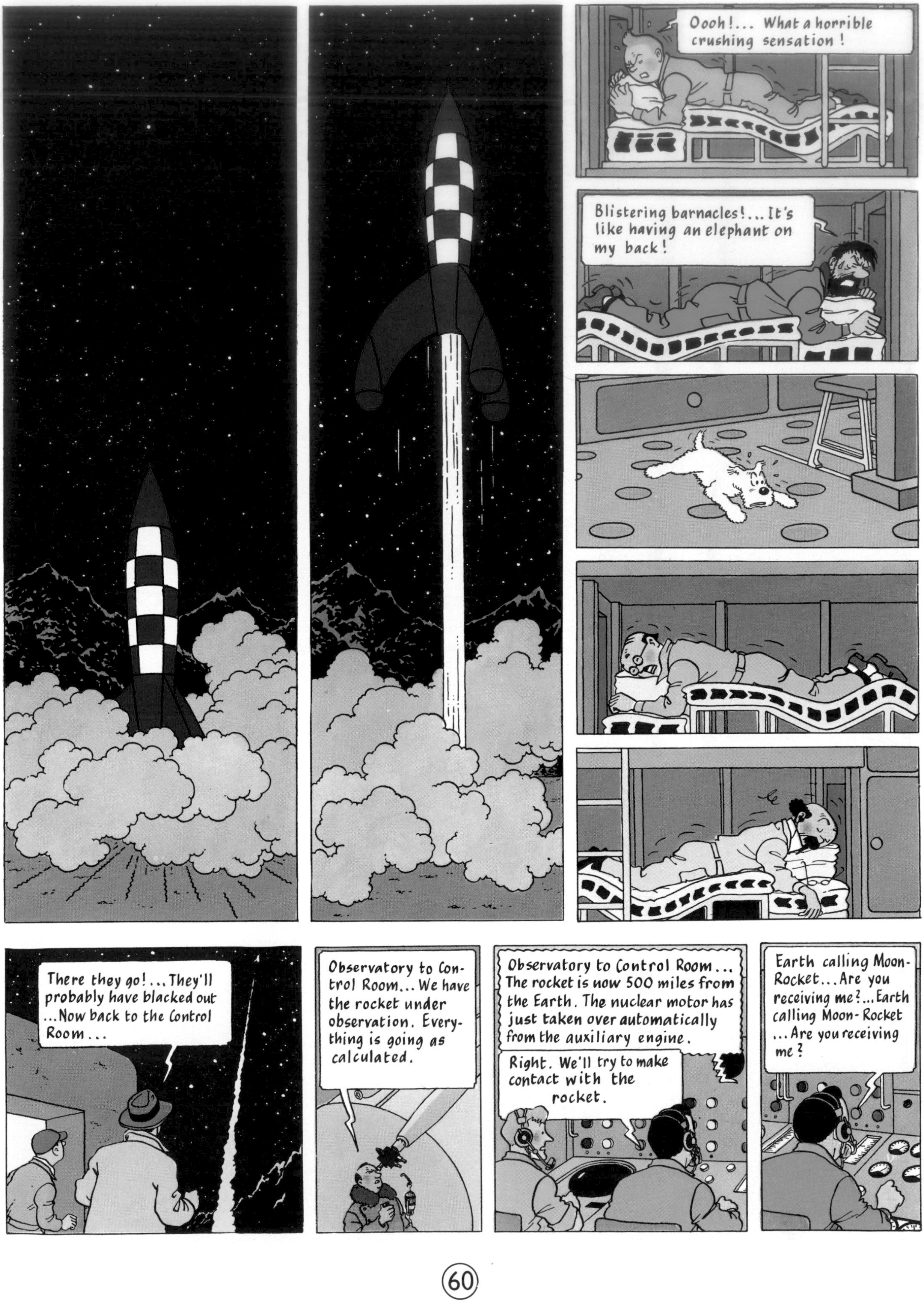

Oooh!... What a horrible crushing sensation!
Blistering barnacles!... It's like having an elephant on my back!
There they go!... They'll probably have blacked out ...Now back to the Control Room...
Observatory to Control Room... We have the rocket under observation. Everything is going as calculated.
Observatory to Control Room... The rocket is now 500 miles from the Earth. The nuclear motor has just taken over automatically from the auxiliary engine.
Right. We'll try to make contact with the rocket.
Earth calling Moon-Rocket... Are you receiving me?... Earth calling Moon-Rocket ...Are you receiving me?

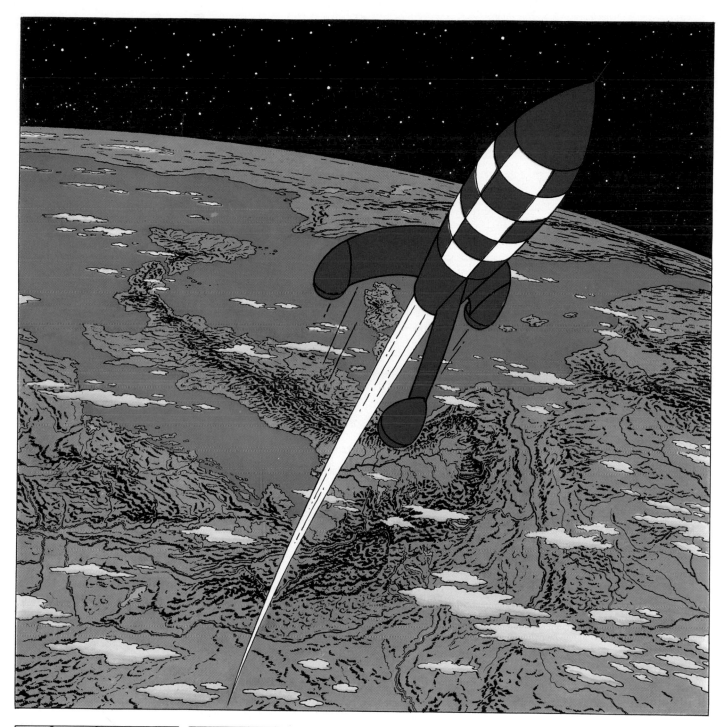

Earth calling Moon-Rocket ... Are you receiving me ? ... Are you receiving me ? ...

Observatory to Control Room...The rocket's altitude is now 1000 miles. Have you succeeded in establishing radio contact yet? Please report ...

Earth calling Moon-Rocket... Are you receiving me? ... Earth calling Moon-Rocket ...

Control Room to Observatory...The Moon-Rocket is not answering.

Earth calling Moon-Rocket...Are you receiving me ? ... Earth calling...

By Lucifer! Surely nothing can have gone wrong?

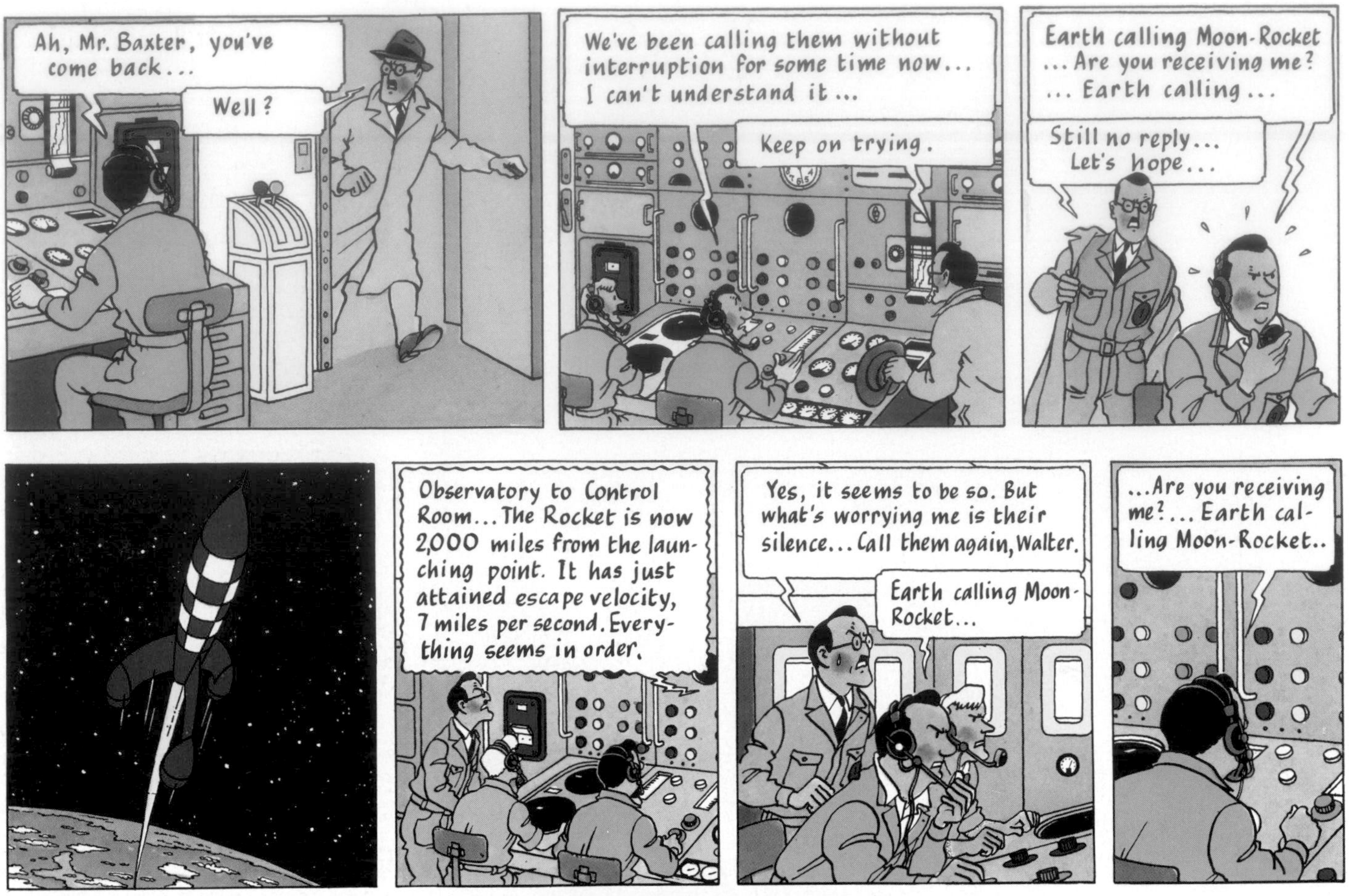
Ah, Mr. Baxter, you've come back...
Well?
We've been calling them without interruption for some time now... I can't understand it...
Keep on trying.
Earth calling Moon-Rocket ... Are you receiving me? ... Earth calling ...
Still no reply... Let's hope...
Observatory to Control Room... The Rocket is now 2,000 miles from the launching point. It has just attained escape velocity, 7 miles per second. Everything seems in order.
Yes, it seems to be so. But what's worrying me is their silence... Call them again, Walter.
Earth calling Moon-Rocket...
...Are you receiving me?... Earth calling Moon-Rocket..

What dangers await Tintin and his friends on the Moon?

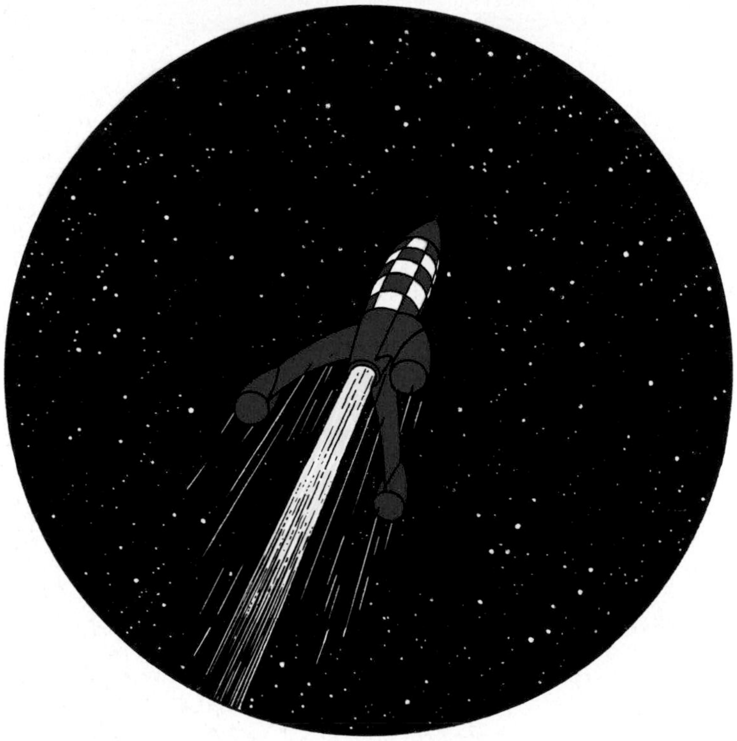

What will happen on this perilous journey into space?

Will they ever return to Earth? You can join in the rest of their great adventure when you read

EXPLORERS ON THE MOON